BY POPULAR DEMAND!
More About the Kids Who
Captured Your Heart in
Love at First Sight.

Todd put his hand gently under Heidi's chin and turned her face up to press his mouth to hers very tenderly. Her lips were smooth but cold and salty. Then he could feel her answering pressure, as if she had been waiting for his kiss. She snuggled closer to him.

"Oh, Todd," she said. "I didn't mean to be so gloomy. I just got scared for a minute, but it's okay now. Being close to you makes it better."

Todd was overcome with love for her and kissed her again. This time her lips were warm and responsive. . . .

Dear Readers,

We at Silhouette would like to thank all our readers for your many enthusiastic letters. In direct response to your encouragement, we are now publishing *three* FIRST LOVEs every month.

As always FIRST LOVEs are written especially for and about you—your hopes, your dreams, your ambitions.

Please continue to share your suggestions and comments with us; they play an important part in our pleasing you.

I invite you to write to us at the address below:

Nancy Jackson
Senior Editor
Silhouette Books
P.O. Box 769
New York, N.Y. 10019

BE MY
VALENTINE
Elaine Harper

First Love from Silhouette

Published by Silhouette Books New York

America's Publisher of Contemporary Romance

Other First Loves by Elaine Harper

Love at First Sight
We Belong Together

SILHOUETTE BOOKS, a Simon & Schuster Division of
GULF & WESTERN CORPORATION
1230 Avenue of the Americas, New York, N.Y. 10020

ISBN: 0-671-53339-8

First Silhouette Books printing February, 1983

10 9 8 7 6 5 4 3 2 1

America's Publisher of Contemporary Romance

Printed in the U.S.A.

To Brian—
To Celebrate His Graduation

1

Todd Roberts was watching from his upstairs window when the mailman's truck rattled down Marigold Lane and stopped at the Robertses' mailbox. Maybe today he would hear from Janine. He hurtled down the stairs, eager to reach the mailbox before his younger sister, Sandy, or his mother did. If Janine did write him, he didn't want anybody to know about it.

Sprinting down the front sidewalk, Todd thought about the letter he had written to her. Janine's best friend, Sarah, had given him Janine's address in Uruguay, where she was Blossom Valley High's exchange student. When Sarah gave him the address, she told him cautiously: "You know that Janine was pretty much going steady with Craig Matthews when she left. He saw her off at the plane and all."

"Yeah," Todd had answered, "but I just wanted to

write and thank her for helping me get elected president of the senior class."

"She'll be glad to get a letter from home," Sarah had answered. "Frankly, I think she's getting homesick. Kind of tired of talking Spanish all the time and eating *frijoles*."

But despite Craig Matthews, Todd had written his heart out to Janine, because of the lonely summer. He had told her she was the only girl he had ever liked, and that he wanted to take her to the first school dance after she returned from South America. That had been several weeks ago, and he could expect a reply by now. Craig Matthews might forget about Janine when he went off to college, and then she would be Todd's girl.

Todd impatiently scooped the mail out of the box. There was a *National Geographic,* a couple of bills, a letter to his mother from Aunt Margaret, a sample of a new kind of cold pill, some sweepstakes announcements, and a letter to Sandy from one of her girlfriends who had moved away during the summer. Todd went through the whole pile of mail again to make sure Janine's reply was not stuck on the back of some other letter. It would probably be one of those thin blue airmail letters, which could easily be lost.

Todd ambled slowly back up the walk, feeling empty and neglected. With a lot of his friends off on vacation, it was a boring summer. The Robertses had not gone anywhere except up to Uncle Henry and Aunt Margaret's cottage at Lake Tahoe for a week. Todd would be glad when school started again and things got going.

Halfway up the walk, Todd heard a weird sound, a loud flapping and swooshing noise. Something like a UFO darted past him, almost grazing his hair, and causing him to duck down and scatter mail all over the ground. It was unnatural and scary. He

8

felt a rush of air, as from another planet, about him.

What he saw next was just about unbelievable. There were these three giant birds coming in for a landing on his lawn: a huge blue one and two bronzy blue ones not quite so large. They had little crests on their heads, and they strutted majestically about the edges of the Robertses' lawn, searching for seeds and insects and gulping down Mrs. Roberts' pansies. Todd realized they were peacocks! Sandy barged out the front door with her friend Vicky.

"Do you believe this?" Sandy demanded.

"It blows me away," Vicky replied.

"They must have escaped from some zoo," Todd speculated. "I guess they're peacocks, but they look kind of scraggly."

Mrs. Kendall, the next-door neighbor, who was out cutting roses, looked over in surprise and came through the gate in the hedge to watch the peacocks.

"Almost scalped me," Todd said and grinned at Mrs. Kendall.

A couple of kids on small bikes stopped in front of the Roberts house, watching the huge birds with delight. They rode off at top speed and soon returned with three companions. The crowd thickened around the Robertses' lawn.

"What should we do?" Mrs. Roberts asked. "They must belong to somebody."

"I'd call the SPCA," said Mr. Conroy, the neighbor on the other side.

"Todd, you go call the SPCA," Mrs. Roberts directed, as a purple pansy disappeared down a long blue neck.

"Peacocks? Sounds like a cock and two hens," the voice from the SPCA began. "Well, that's got to be the Holmstroms' birds. They're quite the wanderers. We get several calls every year about them. So I keep their number. Hold on."

Todd wrote down the phone number. It was in an adjoining suburb, not too far away. He dialed the number and told the female voice that answered that the three peacocks were in his yard.

"Those little vagrants!" the voice exclaimed. "What's your address? We'll be right over to pick them up."

On his way back out of the house, Todd grabbed a box of puffed rice. Scattered around the yard, it might keep the peacocks from eating the pansies and also keep the birds there until their owners arrived.

The word spread around the neighborhood that there were these peacocks on the Robertses' lawn, and kids and parents came from way down the block to see them, in wagons, on trikes. There were even babies in strollers.

"Hey, don't get too close," Todd yelled at the crowd. "You might scare them away before the owners get here. And get that dog out of here. He'll panic those birds," he scowled at a bystander.

"Come on, Roscoe," the dog's owner urged, moving on. But other people kept coming.

"Where're their fantails?" one boy asked.

"Their tails are all raggedy. Somebody must have plucked out the feathers," another speculated.

When the peacock owner's station wagon pulled up in front of the Roberts house, a lot of kids on bikes had to get out of the driveway to make room for them to park. A girl sprang out of the front seat and ran toward the peacocks. The largest bird took off and flew up onto Mrs. Kendall's roof.

"Jupiter, you naughty boy!" the girl exclaimed, her hands on her hips, looking up at the roof. The two peahens kept pecking at the puffed rice Todd had scattered.

Todd looked at the peacock owner in astonishment. He had never seen such a girl anywhere. Her long smooth hair was a whitish-blonde, but she had dark brows and eyes that shone with merriment as she scolded Jupiter the peacock. An engaging dimple appeared in her cheek as she turned, laughing, toward the two peahens, and Todd noticed the freshness and sparkle of her skin.

"Who was it that called us?" the girl asked.

"It was me," Todd answered with alacrity, and then, feeling awkward at his grammatical gaffe before the sparkling beauty, he added, "I, that is," and then wished he had not. He stole a look at her lithe, slender body in white slacks with a blue-and-white striped tank top. She had all the right curves.

"Well, I must apologize for these rambling rascals," she said. "Every now and then they get restless and take off."

By now a tall, athletic-looking tanned blond man had emerged from the station wagon, opened the hatchback, and approached the birds in a relaxed manner.

"You get Hera, Dad, and I'll get Juno," the girl said in an efficient, self-confident voice. The man and the girl approached the peahens calmly, encircling them with their arms and carrying them to the back of the station wagon. There were three crates in the car, and they put one bird in each of the first two, clamping down the corners, which had holes for the peacocks' necks to stick out. Their little crests quivered as their heads darted nervously about.

"We have to put them in crates so they won't jump around the car and damage their feathers." The girl smiled at an open-mouthed boy who stood by the station wagon.

The girl's father—Mr. Holmstrom, Todd guessed —was making clucking peacock noises at the cock on the roof next door.

"Don't trample the flowers!" Mrs. Kendall cautioned as the crowd moved through the gate in the hedge into her yard.

The cock squawked at Mr. Holmstrom and started pecking in the rain gutters, making loud metallic noises.

"I could go up and get him if I had a ladder," Todd offered.

"There's a ladder out in the garage," Mrs. Kendall offered, and Todd ran for it. If he could catch the cock, he might make an impression on this incredible girl.

Todd leaned the ladder up against the Kendall house and scrambled up as fast as he could, hoisting himself onto the roof. He crawled cautiously across the shingles, conscious that a sea of expectant faces was raised to watch him.

Todd inched up on the peacock, and just as he almost had him in his grasp, the peacock uttered a squawk and escaped to look cagily down at Todd from a perch in a tall eucalyptus tree.

Todd was humiliated. He looked like a fool, having been outwitted by the disdainful bird. The crowd had all turned their faces from him and up into the eucalyptus tree.

Todd saw his father drive up. Todd's father worked at a bank and came home early. Mr. Roberts, confused, scrutinized the crowd milling about the yard and the station wagon blocking the driveway, with the peacock heads protruding from the crates. Todd was crawling back over Mrs. Kendall's roof and reaching his leg down to feel for a rung of the ladder. All he needed now was to have the ladder fall out from under him to make him look more foolish. The Holmstrom girl filled his thoughts. Once back on the ground, viewing the throng that milled from his yard to the Kendalls', his eyes sought the peacock's lovely owner like a leaf being pulled into a whirlpool. He couldn't keep from staring at her. Mr. Holmstrom was still making his clucking noises at the peacock, but the bird only peered at him from his superior position in the tree.

"Why don't we just leave him here, Dad?" the girl said in her crisp, efficient voice. "If we take Juno and Hera home, he'll probably follow us, or at least he'll come home at nightfall."

"Good idea, Heidi," her father agreed. "Let's just leave the old rogue to find his own way home."

"It's their habit to come home to roost," Mr. Holmstrom explained to Todd, whose eyes moved reluctantly from their contemplation of Heidi. "Don't worry. I think you'll be rid of him within a few hours."

Another car inched its way to the curb in front of the Roberts house, and Mrs. Van Arsdale got out. She was the mother of Todd's friend Art, and she had brought some pelargonium cuttings to Mrs. Roberts.

"What's the matter here?" she asked Mr. Roberts in alarm as she walked across the lawn. "Has there been an accident?"

"No," laughed Mr. Roberts. "There just seems to be a peacock up in the eucalyptus tree."

"A peacock? Well, what next!" Mrs. Van Arsdale peered up into the tree and then looked back down toward Todd. "Well, Todd!" she exclaimed. "What's happened to you? You must have grown half a foot since I saw you last. Must have been last spring since you've been around to the house."

"Not quite half a foot, but must be three or four inches," Mr. Roberts said proudly. "Late bloomer, I guess. He's looking down on me now. We were beginning to think he was going to be a runt, and here he had this spurt of growth. It's lucky he works down at the pizza parlor. Otherwise, he'd be eating us out of house and home." Mr. Roberts laughed his loud and hearty laugh.

Todd looked uncomfortably at Heidi. He wished she were not hearing all these intimate family details about him, that she could think he had always been tall.

"Well, some of them don't stop growing until they get to be twenty-one," Mrs. Van Arsdale gabbled on. "I believe you've outstripped Art by now, Todd. He'll be surprised to see how you've changed. Gets back from visiting his cousin in Texas this Friday."

"Why don't they have fantails like in the pictures?" a little girl was asking Heidi.

"They molt their train feathers at this time of year, and then they grow in fresh, new ones so they'll always be beautiful," Heidi explained. "Their trains won't be fully grown back until after Christmas. Then Jupiter will start strutting around and displaying his fan."

"The fan is not really a tail," Heidi's father added. "Their tails are really some little stiff brown feathers that hold the train in place."

Todd felt a hand press softly on his arm and turned to look into the animated dark eyes of Heidi Holmstrom. The touch of her hand sent a kind of pleasurable jolt through him. "Well, thanks for everything—for letting us know where they were. I hope they didn't do much damage, but it looks as if your pansy border is a little worse for the experience. I wish we could keep them from wandering around and pestering people. But the only way we could do it would be to clip their wings, and, well . . ."

"No, you wouldn't want to do that," Todd said, bemused by her dimples and the incredible clarity of her skin. "Besides, it wasn't any trouble. In fact, just the opposite."

Heidi's eyes twinkled in amusement, and Todd felt a flush coming over his face. Heidi only pressed her little white hand against his arm and said, "Thanks again."

Her father came over and pumped Todd's hand in a strong grip, echoing Heidi's thanks. "Now if that vagabond keeps hanging out at your place, just give us a call tomorrow. Here's my card. But I think we'll see old Jupiter back at our house before too long. Sorry to have disturbed you."

Mr. Roberts came over and shook hands with Mr. Holmstrom, and Heidi and her father got in the car, which was backed down the driveway.

Everyone looked after them and then up into the tree to see if Jupiter would follow them, but he only sat majestically among the dark cascading leaves of the eucalyptus, as if he were accustomed to presiding over such a spectacle as the one he viewed on the Robertses' lawn. But now the crowd began to disperse. Todd looked down at the card in his hand and saw Heidi's father's name: Neilson Holmstrom, Ph.D., Professor of Biology. He taught at the state college. They probably kept the peacocks for observation.

Todd went into his house, trailing behind his dad and Mrs. Van Arsdale with her pelargonium cuttings. He had picked up all the mail, which was dirty and trampled on. The sample of cold medicine had been ground into the walk, so that the tablets were broken. Todd threw it into the wastebasket. He scowled as he reached the door of his room. It was open, and as he appeared, Sandy and Vicky darted out.

"What are you doing in my room?" he demanded. "You know my room is off limits."

"We were just in there because we could see the peacocks better from your room than mine," Sandy replied. Vicky simpered and rolled her eyes at Todd. Sandy's friends were always peeking out at him from Sandy's room and giggling, or contriving to come into the kitchen when he was there with one of his friends. But to have those silly brats invading his room was too much. Had they seen anything he didn't want them to see? For instance, the picture of the calendar girl he had gotten from Steve Atkins. Steve had been over the night before and had left a can of beer in Todd's room. If Sandy and Vicky saw it, they would tell his parents, and they would have a heart attack. There was no privacy. Todd saw with relief that the beer can was behind his desk, where it probably would not have been seen, but he was going to have to get a lock put on his door anyway.

Todd didn't have much to do until he went down to work at the pizza parlor later in the afternoon. He took his skateboard and went to the driveway. He did a few turns, and then Vicky and Sandy came out with skateboards to join him. Vicky kept sidling glances at him and making Todd feel self-conscious, so he quit and went back into the house again, inspecting himself in the hall mirror as he passed by. It was true, he had changed quite a bit in the past summer. He beetled his eyebrows and glowered at himself, then struck a few other poses, tough ones and dramatic ones. He leaned his hand on his chin and could feel the bristles. He could easily grow a mustache or a beard now, but people didn't wear them in high school. Maybe when he was in college next year. He wondered how he would look with a mustache. He went in the bathroom, locked the door, got his mother's eyebrow pencil, and drew himself a mustache. He would look pretty fierce with one. He washed that one off and drew one in a different shape that drooped down over the corners of his mouth, so that he looked like a riverboat gambler in a movie. His face was getting a little more angular than it had been last year, and his nose didn't look quite so snubby. He wondered what impression he had made on Heidi Holmstrom.

There was a pounding on the bathroom door. "You've been in there practically all afternoon," Sandy complained.

"Get lost," Todd replied, hastily soaping off his gambler's mustache. Then he came out, sweeping by Sandy and the everlastingly giggly Vicky. In his room, he surveyed the girl on the calendar poster critically. She didn't measure up to Heidi Holmstrom. Heidi was a real knockout, but not flamboyant. She was too natural and fresh-looking to be showy or conspicuous; she was really original, not like any girl or movie star Todd had seen. She had her own unique quality and a no-nonsense way about her—like when she had zeroed in on that peacock; also, when she had put her hand on his arm. He had never seen a girl do that, especially on such short acquaintance. When she had touched him, an aura of warmth and sincerity radiated from her. She was just about the most unaffected girl Todd had ever seen. He hoped the peacock—Jupiter —wouldn't go home, so he would have to call her the next day.

Todd looked out the window and saw Steve Atkins riding up on his bike. As Todd went to let him in, he yelled through Sandy's door, "One of my friends is coming over, and I don't want you barging into my room to pretend to get records or anything."

Sandy would be a sophomore when school started, and Todd predicted she and her friends would be quite a trial to him this year, always bugging him. He was going to be president of the senior class and wouldn't want any embarrassing incidents to happen while he was.

As Todd and Steve went down the hall, the two tittering girls peeped out, and the boys ducked into the bedroom, closing the door. They played a few records, and Steve drank the can of beer he had hidden there.

"Take the can out with you. My mom will blow her top if she finds it in here," Todd said. Since he had been elected class president, he felt uncomfortable about doing forbidden things like sneaking beers. It seemed as if a president had to be a model of propriety, and as the opening day of school approached, Todd felt apprehensive. What had he gotten himself in for when he ran for election?

"Art will be back on Friday. We're going to have an end-of-summer celebration Saturday night," Steve told Todd. "Sarah was the one that suggested it. It'll be at her house. Jennifer Baines will be your date, and Connie Campbell will be Art's."

"Jennifer Baines?" Todd objected. "How did you pick her for me?"

"She told Sarah she liked you and asked her to fix her up with you."

"Yeah," Todd said cynically. "Last year Jennifer Baines turned up her nose every time she met me in the hall. The year before, too, for that matter."

"Well, since you got to be president of the class, all the girls will probably want to date you. Who knows? Maybe you might really like her once you get to know her. Besides, Sarah has it all set up."

"Sarah has gotten very bossy since she became class secretary. I wish I hadn't put her on the slate."

"Come on, Todd. Be a sport."

"Are you and Sarah going steady or something?"

"We never have exactly said we were, only I always go out with her, and she never goes out with anybody but me. It's too bad Janine is down in South America. If she were here, we could get her."

"Would I have to go over to Jennifer's house and pick her up and bring her home, or would she already be there?"

"You should pick her up, I guess."

Todd frowned. Somehow, going by her house to get her and meet her parents and all seemed to entangle him, to impose a responsibility he hadn't asked for. He thought of the girl Heidi, who had appeared at his house that afternoon, sort of on a whirl of peacock wings. Now if it had only been her . . .

"I'll think about it and let you know later." Todd started to tell Steve about Heidi, and then he didn't. Heidi now seemed unreal, kind of like those mythological characters who disappeared up into the sky and became constellations—someone he had imagined, from a fabulous world, another planet.

"There were these weird peacocks that came over into our yard this afternoon," he told Steve.

"Peacocks!"

"Yeah, they belonged to some biology professor from State. He came over to get two of them." Todd was very conscious of the important gap in his story, and he remembered the pressure of her hand on his arm and her face looking into his, only about eighteen inches away. "One of them might still be around. Look. Out in the eucalyptus." Todd was afraid it was gone, but a minute inspection of the large leafy tree revealed a gleam of iridescent blue.

Todd and Steve went down into the yard. Steve picked up a pebble and tossed it into the eucalyptus tree to see if he could flush the peacock out.

"Don't do that!" Todd yelled with sudden anger. "You might hurt him, and this professor would be really mad." Todd wished Jupiter would just live in the tree, so Heidi would have to come back.

Todd and Steve shot a few baskets out by the

garage. They could see Vicky and Sandy peering out the window at them.

"I can't get over how much you grew this summer," Steve panted as they paced around the driveway in front of the basketball hoop. "I bet if you had gotten your height before this year, you could have been on the basketball team."

"Maybe so." Todd recalled with a little misgiving how Janine, the girl he had liked last year, had been snatched away by the star basketball player, Craig Matthews. If Todd had been on the team, would Janine have liked him better? Todd put the thought out of his mind. It didn't seem to matter so much anymore whether Janine liked him or not. He and Steve got back to back and determined that Todd was more than an inch and a half taller than Steve.

"You must be the tallest one of our gang now," Steve said with a shade of misgiving, "only when you grow that much all at once, it makes you pretty skinny." He contemplated Todd's lanky, slender frame.

"Let's go in and see if we can find Dad's old barbells," Todd said, opening the garage door. "We could work out a little with them. Maybe I'll go out for track in the spring."

They found the barbells and did a little lifting, then Steve had to go home for dinner, and Todd had to get ready for his job at the pizza parlor.

"You've got to tell me whether you're going to Sarah's party for Art," Steve pressed him as he left.

"I'll only go if Jennifer Baines is already at Sarah's, and I don't have to pick her up *or* take her home," he grimaced.

"Okay then, I'll tell Sarah."

Todd watched Steve disappear down the block on his bike. Sarah Sampson really had Steve under her thumb. Todd would not want to get roped in like that, unless it was by some really super girl like Heidi Holmstrom. Images of Heidi running across his lawn after Juno and Hera filled his thoughts as he went up to get ready to go to the pizza parlor. It was pleasant to think about her. It made all his troubles and responsibilities fade into the woodwork. As he opened his door, he saw an envelope on his desk that hadn't been there before. Todd picked it up angrily. Those little creeps had invaded his room again. He opened the envelope.

"Vicky wants to know if you like her." It was written on a piece of Sandy's stationery with her name and pictures of flowers around the edges. "Check one of these squares: ☐ A lot ☐ Sort of ☐ Not yet."

What was he going to be asked to endure next? First that snooty Jennifer Baines and now the infant, Vicky. Todd snatched the cap off a ball-point pen and scrawled across the note: "Bug off and keep out of my room." He tossed the envelope scornfully through Sandy's door as he passed down the hall. Then he leaped down the stairs two at a time.

"Bye, Mom, I'm leaving," he said. The sun was setting as he went out the front door. The sky was all streaked with red-and-gold clouds like a Fourth of July display. As he sprinted down the walk toward the pizza parlor where he worked, he heard a rustling in the eucalyptus tree, and he knew Jupiter was moving against the dry, peeling bark and among the long festoons of blue-gray leaves. Then he heard a loud rattling noise, and he saw the majestic bird glide out over the red spangled sky. It was an awesome sight to view Jupiter silhouetted against the sunset, his wings awkwardly bearing up his heavy body as he flapped toward the west. Going home to roost. Home to Heidi—the lucky bird. Todd could imagine Heidi's small white hand stroking the bird's richly colored feathers. Now there was nothing left at Todd's house to testify to that enchanted hour when the peacocks had visited the Robertses. Todd felt a melancholy pang as Heidi assumed the substance of a dream.

2

Todd slipped on his white apron and chef's cap, and a couple of guys grinned at him from the counter in front of the oven where they put the sauce, cheese, sausage, mushrooms, and other ingredients on the pizzas. "The doughboy has arrived. On with the show!" one of them yelled.

Todd was the one who threw the pizza dough up in the air to make the crusts. He did it in a display window to attract customers. People would approach the window with big smiles, expecting Todd to do some clowning around with the dough. Todd had a reputation for being a prankster and showman. He had been tossing the pizza dough for several months now, and he was tired of doing it.

"Can't I trade with one of the inside guys, just assembling the pizzas and cashiering?" he asked the manager.

The manager didn't take him seriously. He only grinned. People always smiled when they saw Todd, expecting him to put on a comical act. "But you're our big drawing card. People come from all over the county to watch your performance."

Todd thought that was an exaggeration, but he had to admit that his clowning and showing off had gotten him elected president of the senior class. And now, his exalted office made him conspicuous enough. When school started on Monday, he would probably get enough attention because of being one of the school's big wheels that he wouldn't have to think of ways to be funny anymore. Besides, juggling that dough took a lot of energy. Last winter he had worked out a routine where he could have two pizza crusts spinning around at once, but tonight, Todd was only going to put one pizza crust in the air at a time. As the passersby stopped to watch him, they always smiled in anticipation of a good show. Once he had even let a piece of pizza dough fall on his head like a wig, and he had worn it all evening, though it had gotten dry and hard at the end and had kind of stuck to his hair. He got a lot of laughs that night, and the proprietor didn't mind the wasted dough. Anything to draw crowds to the pizzeria. Todd imagined Heidi Holmstrom coming to his window. What would she think of him? Probably that he was a weird ham actor. Heidi was pretty businesslike. Todd had been impressed with the way she addressed her dad, kind of as an equal. He wondered how old she was. It was hard to tell about girls. About sixteen, he would guess. She came up just past his shoulder, and her hands were very small in comparison to his. He wondered where she went to school. He surely would have noticed her if she had gone to Blossom Valley High. She probably went to Orchard High, which was the arch-rival of Blossom Valley in athletics.

Another thing about working in the pizzeria was

that you had to stand up all the time, and Todd's feet would be aching by the end of the evening.

A lot of the kids from his school came in during the evening, and sometimes they would yell, "Hi, Prez." Everyone thought it was a riot that Todd was president of the senior class. Whenever Todd had a good supply of pizza crusts, he could occasionally come over and talk to the customers. Steve came in with some friends during the evening.

"Sarah said it was okay not to pick up Jennifer," he told Todd. "She'll have kind of an end-of-summer slumber party for the girls, and us guys will just come over."

"Okay, I guess," Todd said without enthusiasm, "since it's my Saturday night off. But I could think of better ways to spend it, like you, me, and Art, and some of the other guys playing poker . . ." Without saying it, Todd thought, or taking Heidi Holmstrom to the movies.

"You want to go out with me tomorrow and look for cars?" Todd asked.

"Is your dad going to let you get one?"

"I might be able to talk him into it if I found a good one. I have a lot of money saved up." Todd pictured himself driving up to the high school in a shiny powder-blue convertible such as Quentin Pierce, the lead in most of the school musicals, drove. He pictured Heidi, with her pale blonde hair, riding in it.

Todd and Steve explored the used car lot on Saturday, but none of the cars within Todd's price range would do. Todd talked to his father that afternoon about adding to his money, arguing that the president of the senior class should have his own set of wheels. "I'll probably have all kinds of business I have to do for the class, and I have to have a way to get around," he wheedled.

"Buying a car is only the beginning," his father lectured Todd. "After that, you have to have insurance, which for a teenager is astronomically high. And you have to buy gas and have the car maintained. The mechanics charge an arm and a leg for everything."

"I could take a course in auto mechanics," Todd pleaded.

"We'll talk about it again after you do," his father told him. "Meanwhile, you'll just have to take your turn with the family car."

Todd decided to walk over to Sarah Sampson's party that night. If he didn't go over with Steve or Art, he could take off whenever he pleased if that Jennifer Baines got too pushy. When Todd arrived, they were starting a fire in the barbecue grill on the patio, and everyone was going to assemble his own shish kebab to cook. Maybe it wouldn't be so bad, after all. There were eight people at the party. There was a horseshoe-pitching setup in the back of the yard, and they tossed horseshoes for a while until the coals developed a gray ash around them with a fiery ember showing through. Todd was ravenous, and everybody kidded him about how many shish kebabs he ate. The air was filled with an enticing aroma of cooking meat. The girls had been there early, and they had made a big chocolate cake. Todd felt pretty mellow after such a filling meal.

"We're going in to play some records in the family room and dance now," Sarah announced.

"I heard you were a cool dancer," Jennifer said to Todd. "Didn't you win the pumpkin at the Halloween mixer last year?"

"Yeah," Todd admitted modestly. "Only I had more energy last year. This year I'm older and tireder."

Everyone laughed at that, and then they all

danced. Jennifer was getting pretty possessive of Todd when they stopped dancing and sat down to talk.

"Hey, I had a letter from Janine Anderson from Uruguay this week," Sarah told them.

"How does she like it down there?" Connie asked.

"She says it's really interesting, though she misses being here. This family she lives with—the father is in a leather-processing business. Uruguay seems to be a big cattle-raising country."

"Where is Uruguay, anyway?" Art asked.

"It's kind of wedged in between Brazil and Argentina, on the east coast of South America. It's a pretty small country," Sarah said. "Janine and I looked it up in the atlas when she first heard she was going there."

"It must be really weird to live in a country where you don't know a single person, with a perfectly strange family, where they don't even speak your language," Jennifer commented.

"Yeah, unreal," Connie agreed.

"She has about three more months to stay," Sarah said. "She'll be back around Christmas."

"Why don't we have a welcome-back New Year's Eve party?" Jennifer suggested. "My folks would let me have it at our house. You're all invited." She looked meaningfully at Todd.

"You would have to invite Craig Matthews, too," Connie remarked. "I heard Janine and Craig got really thick before she left, and that he even gave her his class ring, just as her plane was about to leave."

"That's true. Since Janine and I were best friends, I saw her off, too, and they got into such a clincher at the end that I thought Janine was going to miss the plane. They practically couldn't tear themselves apart, and Craig was really depressed when the plane took off."

Sarah cast a glance at Todd, to see what his reaction was, because she knew Todd had been hung up on Janine the year before.

He met Sarah's glance and twisted uncomfortably in his chair. Even if he had chased after Janine last year, he didn't seem to care that much this year. He was pretty much losing interest.

"They'll probably be steadies this year," Art commented.

"But he's over at Berkeley in college," Connie said, sighing, for Craig Matthews had been the school heartthrob the year before.

"Just imagine," Sarah said. "We'll be the oldest ones in school this year, the top of the heap."

"Yeah, the seniors," Steve added. "And Todd, here, is the top dog, the president of the class."

Todd felt uncomfortable again, under their scrutiny.

"What are you going to do for us, Todd?" Jennifer asked.

"We want lots of parties," Connie demanded.

"You should declare every Friday a holiday for seniors," Art suggested.

"And seniors can get in front of anyone they like in the cafeteria line," Sarah added.

Todd listened to their comments with increasing discomfiture. He was not sure just what he was supposed to do as president. He had talked briefly to the president of last year's class, but didn't learn much from the conversation.

"This year we have to decide where we're going to college," Sarah reminded them.

"We have to take the Scholastic Aptitude Tests," Jennifer groaned.

"Yeah, if you don't do well in those, you might not even get into college," Todd said, thinking with some misgiving of his spotty grade record, regretting for the moment that he had spent a lot of time fooling around and thinking of ways to be the funny guy in his classes instead of getting good grades.

"Where do you think you'll go, Todd?" Jennifer asked.

"I might go down to State."

"State! But that's too close. It wouldn't be like going to college at all. I want to go someplace really far away, where my parents won't always be on my back. Like down to San Diego, for instance."

"Well, I was thinking about specializing in biology. There is this cool biology professor at State. Neilson Holmstrom, Ph.D."

"I didn't know you had taken biology."

"I haven't yet, but I'm about to take it this year."

"Are you going to be a doctor or something?"

"Yeah, something like that, I guess." Todd yawned. "I've got to go home. I have to get up early and help my dad with some stuff."

Jennifer looked disappointed.

"Come on, you can stay a little longer," Steve pleaded warily, at a prodding from Sarah.

"Nope. Got to split." And Todd was off, walking through the night, pleased with himself for not getting pressured. On the way home he thought of Heidi Holmstrom and wished he would see her on Monday when school started.

The next week, when Todd looked around Blossom Valley High, it seemed to him that they were letting in people younger and younger. It felt funny not to have people older than himself to look up to. A lot more girls said hi to him this year, stopped him in the hallway to talk, or, if they were in his classes, consulted with him about their lessons. Girls in his classes sometimes flirted with him this year. They never had before. He thought it was just because he was president. Yet when he looked in the mirror, he had to admit that he was getting to be an okay-looking guy as he matured.

One day in the third week of the quarter a message came into his homeroom that he was wanted in the principal's office. From old instinct, Todd felt a sense of apprehension. What had he been caught at now?

Waiting later in the principal's reception room, Todd looked around at the surroundings. They were familiar, for he had been here before. There were colored photographs on the wall of Northern California scenes: Emerald Bay at Lake Tahoe, the Carmel Mission, the autumn colors of the vineyards against the mountains in the wine country.

Todd remembered the last time he had been here. There was this kid who had a hang glider, and he had told Todd he could try it out, but they would have to cut their afternoon classes and go down to Half Moon Bay. It was something Todd could not resist, and then one thing had led to another, and they had to forge absence slips from their parents saying they had gotten sick, and Todd had been in a lot of trouble with his folks, as well as with the principal. Another time Todd smoked a cigarette in the bathroom—the first and last cigarette he had ever tried—but at just that time the vice-principal had come in for an inspection, and there was a big flap about that; and then other times he had been in the principal's office, he had been cutting up in classes and distracting the students. Even Todd's dad had been into the principal's office, defending Todd for being a high-spirited kid who just had too much excess energy. Then there was the time someone had stolen the principal's chair. Todd hadn't had anything to do with that, but he had been a suspect and had been questioned about it.

When Todd was ushered into the principal's office, instead of frowning at him from under his beetling brows, the principal got up and came around his desk and smiled at Todd and shook hands with him.

"Well, Mr. Roberts, I think we have talked before, but this time we meet under more favorable circumstances," he said in a hearty, cordial voice. "I understand you're president of the senior class." He looked rather bemused, as if the fact were something of a marvel.

"Yeah," Todd confirmed, "only I haven't exactly started anything yet."

"Sit down, Mr. Roberts." The principal indicated a chair beside his desk. "I'm glad you haven't, because you and I should discuss it first. We need to have an understanding about the limitations and possibilities of the senior class activities."

"Yes, sir."

"You'll probably be having some social events— dances and the like. Now, functions of this kind must be held on school property. We can't give the impression that something is a school event if it's not held here, where we can exercise some control over it, and where the school's insurance is in effect in case of accident."

"Oh, sure," Todd replied. "We would have anything we planned in the gym or cafeteria or someplace around here."

"And I'll be expecting you to report any planned activities, so that we can coordinate the dates with other projected school events and see that proper supervision can be provided."

"Oh, sure. I would let you know if we planned anything," Todd said, getting a little scared. What all was he expected to plan? Whatever it was would come under the close scrutiny of the principal.

"I would assume you'll soon be holding a senior class meeting to decide on the year's activities," the principal continued.

"Is that the way they do it?" Todd asked.

"Yes. You should announce a meeting of the senior class. You may reserve a classroom for it. Right after school is a good time. Maybe you'd like to set a date for it now, and we can announce it over the P.A. system. You may want to appoint some committees. Perhaps one for social events. Certainly you'll want a committee to take care of graduation activities, and I'm sure your class, like all other classes, will want to perform some service to the school. You could get someone to run a school volunteer bureau that teachers can use when they need someone to help keep order in the cafeteria, help in the library, or run errands."

"Sure." Todd's head was swimming.

"Why don't we look on the calendar and see what other things are planned for after school, and we can arrive at a date by elimination."

They found a Wednesday afternoon when there wasn't too much going on at school and set that as the date for the senior meeting. "You'll need to have an agenda," the principal said.

"An agenda?"

"Yes. A list of the topics you need to bring up at the meeting, so that there won't be anything left unresolved afterward." Todd and the principal worked on a list of things the senior class ought to do during the year, and when they finished the principal shook hands with Todd again. "Well, Mr. Roberts, I'm glad to see you're interested in more worthwhile activities this year in place of your former puerile pursuits. I wish you a very successful year as president."

That was a really unusual experience for Todd, talking man-to-man with the principal. He wished that Neilson Holmstrom, Ph.D., and his daughter, Heidi, could see him now. He thought about the senior class social events. A Valentine dance would be a good idea. He could picture himself escorting Heidi to such an event.

Todd walked through the hallway to his next class, English. The principal had given Todd a late slip with his own signature on it, and Todd felt important giving it to the teacher. After class, he looked up the word "puerile" in the classroom dictionary. It meant "childish." It was Friday, and after class Todd ran into Art at the lockers.

"Hey, Todd," Art said, his eyes lighting up. "Guess what we're going to do tonight."

"Orbit into outer space? How many guesses do I get?" Todd asked.

"We're going to paper Connie Caldwell's house. And guess who's going to help? Hank Jones. He's the discus thrower on the track team! We'll wait until you get off duty at the pizzeria. We'll be over at my house with the paper."

Todd frowned. He wasn't sure he wanted to horse around and get into mischief on Friday nights anymore. "You better go ahead without me. I'm usually tired after work."

"It wouldn't be the same! We need your juggling arm. You're practically the best paper thrower we have."

"But if you have Hank now, he'll be even better."

"Come on, Todd, we need the whole gang. It's no fun if you're not there."

Todd hesitated. After all, if they would be so disappointed . . . and it wasn't illegal or anything, just a harmless prank. "Well, okay. But don't expect me to do anything afterward. We've really gotten busy this week, and I have this big biology test on Monday."

"This is only Friday, for gosh sakes. Who would be studying biology after work on Friday night?"

After work, Todd reluctantly made his way over to

Art's. Why he was doing it, he didn't know. If Art had planned to paper Connie Caldwell's house, that meant he was hung up on her, and before long, he would be going steady with her. Then he would be the one who deserted the gang on Friday night. Art was a pushover for girls who wanted to go steady. Last year he had done the same thing with some creepy girl who had now moved to Los Angeles.

Art, Hank, and Steve were waiting at Art's. They had three six-packs of tissue, and they all proceeded down the street toward the Caldwells'. It was about midnight, and the lights were out in Connie's house. Art yanked the plastic wrap off one of the packs and passed out a roll to each person. Hank pulled back his discus-throwing arm and tossed a roll high up into a pepper tree on Connie's front lawn, leaving a long trail of tissue down the feathery foliage. All the other boys were working on trees of their own, flinging the rolls of paper into the trees that surrounded the house. Todd had chosen a Monterey pine, and he hurled the paper around it until it looked like a snowy Christmas tree. There was a half-moon illuminating the scene, so that the effect of the festoons of white paper on the dark trees was clearly visible. The boys worked stealthily and quietly, moving around the side yard and unlatching the gate into the backyard, decorating the trees there with more skeins of tissue. Todd could hear an occasional burst of suppressed laughter, but everyone was really holding back and working fast and quietly so they wouldn't wake up the Caldwells and get caught in the act.

When all the eighteen rolls of tissue were used up, the boys spilled out of the backyard. Todd looked back at the fantastic scene, the zigzags and curves of tissue paper silhouetted like an abstract art painting against the foliage surrounding the house. They all converged in front and went across the street to survey their handiwork.

"That's the best job we've ever pulled," Art said with satisfaction. Although Todd resolved it was the last time he would paper anyone's house and had a guilty feeling that a president shouldn't have been doing this, he couldn't help feeling exhilarated to see the spectacle they had wrought, to imagine the surprise of the whole neighborhood when it awoke the next morning. At least, he had ended his papering career in a blaze of glory with the most superb job he had ever seen.

"This will blow Connie away!" Art exclaimed.

"You're a fabulous hurler," Todd complimented Hank. "I didn't think anybody could get it over the top of that big pepper tree."

"It's pretty hard. Not enough weight in those paper rolls," Hank commented. Previously Todd had been the star paper thrower. Now that he was retiring, Hank could take his place.

"I wish I could see their faces when they wake up," Art said.

"Yeah, that's the only bad part. We don't get to see the reaction," Steve commented.

"I know what it's like," Todd said, "because our own house was papered once. Some guys in Sandy's class did it. Everybody gets up and looks out the window and sees this unreal scene and pretends to be outraged, only really they think it's cool, because it shows all the neighbors some kid in that house is popular. The only thing is, it's pretty hard getting all the paper out of the trees and might take all day. Once I knew these people whose house got papered, and then it rained and all this tissue got stuck pretty permanently up in their trees. I bet you could still see some of it up there on Parkside Drive."

"We're all going over to my house now," Art decided.

"Not me. I'm going home," Todd said.

"You're really getting to be a drag," Art complained.

"So long," Todd persisted. Tomorrow, he knew, the news would be leaked to Connie that Art was the instigator of the papering, and she and Art would start hanging out together. As Todd walked home, he pictured himself and the gang papering Heidi's house, and he erased the thought from his mind. That would never do. Heidi would think it was puerile. And you wouldn't do that to a biology professor's house, anyway.

Todd had planned to read a little in his biology book that night. He wanted to ace the test on Monday, and he had heard that sometimes your subconscious mind can learn things during the night. Whatever he read before he went to sleep might get implanted in his mind forever. A lot had happened that day, however, and Todd fell asleep after the first paragraph. His biology book fell off the bed with a thud, and he awoke long enough to turn off his bedside lamp and then was deep in slumber again.

In the morning, Todd opened his blinds to a greater surprise than even the Caldwells had in store. Down on the lawn strutted none other than Jupiter the peacock. He had returned! He appeared grander now. His tail feathers were growing in and looked more luxuriant. Todd ran downstairs in his pajamas and grabbed the puffed rice box. He dashed into the front yard and saw the two hens, Hera and Juno, eating pansies. A surge of joy filled him to bursting. He ran upstairs and scrabbled around his desk for Neilson Holmstrom, Ph.D.'s calling card with the phone number on it. There it was, carefully placed in a corner of his top drawer. He had looked at it several times, trying to think of an excuse to use it. He ran into the hallway to the phone.

"Todd, who are you calling at this hour? It's only six-thirty!" his mother called.

"Those peacocks are back!" Todd exclaimed, his voice hoarse with excitement.

"Don't tell me!" Mrs. Roberts exclaimed from her bed. Todd could hear her getting up as the phone rang at the Holmstroms'.

The voice that answered was unmistakably Heidi's, crisp and wide-awake. He was not getting anyone out of bed at the Holmstroms'. Todd was unable to speak for a moment. He was choked with emotion.

"Hello," Heidi said again in a perplexed voice.

"Hi!" Todd managed to croak. "It's Todd Roberts."

"Oh?" Heidi's voice sounded blank. "Did you want to speak to my father? Are you one of the people who's going on the field trip?"

"No," Todd blurted. "I'm the one whose house the peacocks came to a while back. And now they have come here again."

"Oh, now I know you. They are at your house again? Oh, what a nuisance! My dad isn't here. He's gone to collect some people for a field trip. And he has the car. He'll be back, but just for a minute. Then he'll have to leave on the trip. He won't be able to pick them up until late this afternoon."

"Maybe I could bring them over." Todd's pulses were racing at the thought of seeing Heidi, of being connected to her, even, over the telephone wires.

"It would be too hard for you to catch them. Too much trouble."

"I'll try. Why don't you give me your address? I have these big cartons out in the garage, so they wouldn't get hurt. I could get this kid next door to help. I could probably do it without too much trouble."

"Well, if you want, I guess it would be okay," Heidi said slowly and added her address, giving Todd directions to her house.

3

Todd rushed out to the garage to see if the large cardboard boxes were still there. They should be big enough to hold the peacocks. Then he went next door to see if Bobby Kendall was around. Mrs. Kendall was puttering around the kitchen.

"I'd give Bobby a dollar apiece to help me catch the peacocks," Todd said excitedly. Then he noticed with embarrassment that he still had on his pajamas.

"Maybe Bobby wouldn't mind getting up if he thought he was going to earn some money," Mrs. Kendall told Todd. Bobby came out, tousled and rubbing his eyes. "It's too early," he said. "I'm going back to bed."

"I'll give you two dollars apiece," Todd pleaded.

"Maybe for that much."

"You don't need to change," Todd said. "I still have on my pajamas, and I'm kind of in a hurry."

Todd and Bobby approached the peacocks. "We'll catch the cock first. The big one. So he can't fly up on the roof again," Todd decided. He went into the kitchen and got the bread knife and cut an irregular hole in the top of each box. Then he got some heavy paper tape out of the desk drawer and set the boxes out carefully, to be ready for the captured birds. The peacocks grazed peacefully among Mrs. Roberts' flower beds. Todd decided he would be the one to catch the cock. He crept up on it, noticing that Jupiter had wicked-looking, sharp spurs on the backs of his legs.

It was fairly easy. Jupiter just looked curiously at Todd, not expecting anything, and Todd was able to grab him as he had seen Heidi and Mr. Holmstrom doing. He popped Jupiter into the box and fixed Jupiter's tail so it flowed through a slit in the box. Then he tried to get the bird's head through the hole in the lid, but the opening was too small. He yelled at Bobby, "Hey, hold this guy while I cut the hole bigger." While Bobby held down the squawking cock, Todd enlarged the hole and slipped the lid over Jupiter's head, taping the top on. Jupiter looked fairly comfortable. Todd thought impatiently of Heidi. He should be seeing her in about half an hour, if all went well.

While Todd was taping on Jupiter's container, Bobby caught one of the hens, and they got it into another carton while the last hen pecked contentedly. It was a pushover to incarcerate the birds this time—maybe because there wasn't such a crowd watching. Todd opened the garage door and arranged the cartons in the back of the station wagon.

After he paid Bobby, Todd ran upstairs to change out of his pajamas. He couldn't take much time, for the birds were making a terrible fuss out in the car. He got the car keys from his mother.

"You be careful, Todd. Those birds are making such a fuss, they might distract you while you're driving. I can't see why those people couldn't have come to get the birds themselves."

"Her dad was gone with the car," Todd explained hastily.

"Well, you come right back."

On the way over, Todd wished he hadn't had to dress so hurriedly. He could have taken more time with his hair, and he could have shaved and put on some of his dad's after-shave so he would smell nice when he met Heidi. Jupiter's sharp, angry eyes met Todd's in the rearview mirror, and Todd could see the little tufts on top of his crest quivering with indignation.

Following the directions Heidi had given him, Todd went out Berryville Road, past Orchard High. There were a lot of apricot and prune orchards out there to give the high school its name, and some of the trees were bare, but some still had yellow and brown leaves clinging to them, with the pale autumn sun shining through. Todd turned down the road Heidi had indicated in her instructions. The Holmstroms lived in kind of a rural part of the county. The road to their house led through an orchard, and then he saw the sign "Holmstrom" on a mailbox. This neat farmhouse must be theirs. Todd looked at Jupiter in the rearview mirror and wondered why he would want to come into the more crowded suburbs when he had all this space. As he drove up beside the Holmstroms' house, Todd saw another peacock, a beautiful white one.

Heidi must have been looking out the window, because she ran out as soon as Todd stopped the car. Trailing her were two little tow-headed boys about four years old. Twins. They must have been her little brothers. Todd couldn't believe the way she looked. She had her pale hair pulled back and plaited closely to the back of her head, and there was a long braid down her back. She resembled a sculpture you would see on a coin or in one of those Greek art shows. She had on a dark green running suit that made her look really streamlined. To Todd she appeared even more beautiful than she had been over in his yard.

When Heidi saw the peacocks in Todd's cardboard cartons, she burst out into a delighted peal of laughter. Todd got out of the car and stood speechless to be in Heidi's presence. He felt enchanted, as if her laughter was reaching into him as a kind of mystical chant.

"You really made good time. And you have them all. Wait till Dad sees those containers! He'll get a kick out of it."

Todd's voice returned to him. "Maybe we ought to get them out of the boxes. I was hoping that their new tail feathers wouldn't get crushed."

"That was thoughtful," Heidi said, her dark blue eyes looking into Todd's. A warm glow filled Todd at her glance.

Heidi and Todd hoisted the boxes down from the station wagon and tore off the tape, removing the lids over the peacocks' heads. "Actually, these are pretty ingenious," Heidi said. "A lot lighter than those big wooden shipping crates we have. Those were built especially for shipping peacocks."

"That's a neat white peacock," Todd remarked. The big white cock had come up to greet his wandering relatives. "He must be a different variety."

"No, he's the same kind as the others. Just a mutation—an albino," Heidi said in her assured, knowledgeable voice. Todd looked warily at her. She sounded like she might be very smart—a good student. It was curious how he was attracted to brainy girls. Janine, whom he'd chased after last year, was also smart.

Heidi smiled at Todd, her dimples showing. "What a bother we are to you," she said. "You know, these peacocks will always be partly wild. They'll never be completely domesticated like chickens."

"It's really no bother; they're so beautiful," he assured her, staring again into her dark blue eyes, not sure whether he meant her eyes or the peacocks.

"Well, we'll put them into the aviary for punishment," she said. There was a huge wire-enclosed pen in the back of the Holmstroms' yard where a number of weird-looking birds were roosting.

"What are all these?" Todd asked.

"Just some rare birds Dad likes to raise. He studies them."

"What is that one with all the colors?"

"A wood duck. He's gorgeous, isn't he?"

Just then they heard the Holmstroms' station wagon pull up in the drive and two other cars behind it. Heidi's dad sprang out. "We have one more car coming, and then we're all set," he said.

"We're going on a field trip down to Año Nuevo," Heidi explained. "We hope to see the elephant seals."

"The elephant seals!" Todd exclaimed. "I've always heard about them, but never gotten around to seeing them."

"Why don't you come along?" Heidi suggested. "We'll ask Dad." She approached her father. Mr. Holmstrom was now surrounded by a group of students who had emerged from the waiting cars. An attractive blond woman, who had to be Heidi's mother, appeared on the porch with an urn of coffee and a plate of doughnuts.

"Oh, boy, eats!" one of the college students yelled.

"Dad," Heidi asked, "do you know what happened again? Jupiter and his harem went over to that same house and had to be brought back. What's your name?" She turned to Todd.

"Todd Roberts," he said, feeling insignificant. Apparently he hadn't impressed her as she had him.

"Todd here brought them back. And he's never been down to Año Nuevo. Is there room for him? Could he come along?"

Heidi's father frowned. "We're not really supposed to take anyone along who's not enrolled—the school insurance, you know."

Heidi looked disappointed. "Dad, you should see all the trouble he went to. He even made these containers so the peacocks' tails wouldn't be damaged. Come and see."

Todd feared Heidi's father would not think much of his boxes. But Mr. Holmstrom grinned when he saw the big, crude holes in the carton tops. "Pretty clever," he smiled. "Well, Todd, after all the trouble we've caused you, we owe you a trip. I guess I could squeeze you in as my personal guest." Heidi threw her arms around her dad, and it sent a vicarious thrill through Todd.

"Thanks, Dad," she said, turning a brilliant smile on Todd. He felt himself flushing with excitement. Did she really care that much whether he went? She must like him a little.

"I'll get you some binoculars," Heidi said, running into the house. There were four cars going on the field trip, and after the students had coffee and doughnuts, they piled back into the vehicles. They all called Heidi's father "Doctor Holmstrom." Heidi's father looked around through the cars until he found one that wasn't quite full.

"Here, you could take along another passenger, couldn't you?" He motioned Todd in. Todd felt awkward among all the college students, and he wasn't even going to ride in the same car with Heidi.

"Are you in the class?" a rather plump girl asked.

"No, I'm just a friend of Heidi's," Todd mumbled.

"Oh, you must be Joe," someone said. Todd stiffened. Who was Joe? Was that Heidi's boyfriend? The thought made Todd feel lonely and out of place. Everyone pretty much ignored him then. The caravan had to wend its way over the hairpin curves and winding grades of a range of mountains through redwood forests for three-quarters of an hour. Todd wished he could have been sitting beside Heidi, for all these college students were discussing things he didn't know anything about and making him feel insignificant. Once over the mountains, they proceeded down the coast highway, where they caught frequent vistas of the Pacific Ocean and numerous inviting beaches with fringes of surf. Then they all turned into a side road where there was a parking lot and ranger station, and everyone piled out. Todd was eager to get away from his unfamiliar fellow travelers and find Heidi. She was easy to spot because of her pale, silvery-blonde hair.

As Todd approached her, he asked, "Where are the seals?"

"Oh, there you are!" Heidi's dimples captivated him as she cast him a warm, welcoming smile. "I was hoping you and I would ride in the same car."

"Me, too," Todd agreed. "I don't know anybody here except you."

"Here." Heidi reached up her arms to put a pair of binoculars around his neck. She did everything so naturally and easily. He wanted to seize her hands and keep them there. She was totally fascinating.

Heidi's dad arranged everyone in a group and told them what they would see. First, there would be a pond in a meadow, where they would see lots of migratory ducks. After that, they would cross the meadow and view larks and other songbirds, including many varieties of sparrows. Along the cliffs they would encounter sea birds. One rare specimen that

Dr. Holmstrom hoped someone would spot was a harlequin duck. Last, they would proceed to the beach, which was the breeding grounds of the elephant seals.

"Are you into birds?" Heidi asked Todd.

"It looks like I am now," Todd grinned at her, "but if you're asking whether I know anything about them, the answer is no. I take biology at school, but so far we haven't learned anything about birds. Just about ventricles, valves, aortas, trapezoid muscles, and so forth."

Heidi laughed. "Well, this is an ornithology class. But today we won't discuss the birds' insides. We're just identifying them and trying to learn something about their behavior and habitat."

"You aren't in college, are you?" Todd asked cautiously.

Heidi laughed. "Not for a long time. I'm only a junior in high school."

"I'm a senior," Todd said. He wished she knew he was the president of the senior class, but it would sound like bragging for him to say it. Or maybe he was glad she didn't know. He thought of Jennifer Baines and other people who had suddenly turned on to him after he was elected president.

The class started down the trail to the beach. A lot of the college boys hung around Heidi. They called her "Princess" and kidded her about various things. They cracked jokes that Todd was not in on, making him feel out of place again. Once, when they reached a muddy spot in the road, one of the college boys rushed over and scooped Heidi up and carried her across.

This particular college boy irritated Todd because he was evidently a super hotshot who always spotted an interesting bird before anyone else did and would yell it out loudly, calling attention to himself.

"Belted Kingfisher on the piling to the left of the

reeds!" he shouted while they were at the pond, and everyone frantically trained their binoculars on the spot. Some of them, including Dr. Holmstrom, had big spotting scopes on tripods, and people would line up to look through them for a close-up of the bird.

"You should look at the Belted Kingfisher. He is a neat bird," Heidi urged Todd. "You look first, because I've seen it before." She pushed him toward her father's scope, and Todd saw a crested bird with a very large head and a stripe around the middle of his chest.

"Yeah, neat," Todd agreed. "I never saw a bird that close up before." Birds were something Todd had never thought much about, but now they had pretty much changed his life, starting with the peacocks.

Heidi's father was standing beside the scope, and Todd said to him, "I'll probably be coming down to State and taking biology next year."

"Well, you'll have a head start," Dr. Holmstrom commented. Then he raised his voice and told the class about the varieties of ducks, describing the difference between the diving and dabbling ones. He also told them that the mudhens, which were numerous on the lake, were not ducks at all, but were from a different family that did not have webbed feet. Todd scrutinized the surface of the pond, where hundreds of ducks of various colors and shapes floated, quacked, and dived. Around the edges on one side was a tough stand of reeds, and the other bank stretched away in meadows. He turned to Heidi and said, "Your dad knows the names of all these ducks, doesn't he? You probably know them all yourself."

"You would know them, too, if you came out here as often as we do," Heidi said. "This is the best time to see ducks, because they've migrated to California for the winter season. You wouldn't see many in the summer. I'll teach you to recognize a few of them so you'll start knowing them, too." Heidi pointed out some of the more common ducks: the mallard drake with his iridescent banded green neck and the little curlicue feather on his tail; the scaup, with its sides like a sooty snowbank; the bufflehead with a head patterned in black and white. "And then there's the shoveler. You can see how he gets his name." She pointed out a duck with a bill flattened out like a shovel. "Now when we come back by here this afternoon, I'll expect you to recognize all those ducks." She gave him a look of mock severity, and then they both laughed.

"Hey, Heidi, you have a new boyfriend?" One of the girls in the class ogled Todd. "Nice goin'."

Heidi didn't seem embarrassed by that remark. She only looked over at Todd and smiled.

"American Bittern!" the hotshot screamed, "about five feet west of the piling!" Todd wished he had been the one to yell it, because there was a flurry of excitement and activity.

"Get a look at this," Heidi's father admonished everyone. "You may never get another chance to see one. They are very shy and elusive."

"I've never seen one myself. This is an event," Heidi whispered to Todd. She took his arm and pulled him into the line at the scope. Todd felt a pleasant warmth sweeping through him as Heidi pressed close to him in the crowd, waiting for a look through the scope. Her face was touching his shoulder, and he could see the fine pores of her clear skin and the long dark lashes that fringed her indigo-blue eyes. When she looked up at him, he felt he was being pulled into her eyes, that he might fall inside and learn all of her mysteries—her thoughts and her past memories, the things she liked, and all the things that brought on her ready smile. A ripple of pleasure passed through him, and he felt he had entered a new phase of life.

"Hey, get a move on. The bittern will fly away or something," someone in back yelled.

"Not likely. He wouldn't want to expose himself," Dr. Holmstrom said dryly.

Heidi pressed Todd's arm. "It's your turn," she said softly.

Todd looked blindly through the scope. He saw a wild mass of reeds, and in his confusion he jolted the scope away from its focus.

"Hey, you moved it," someone accused. Dr. Holmstrom replaced Todd at the eyepiece and refocused the scope on the bird. Todd was muscled aside as those behind him in the line took their turns. Heidi was peering through now. Todd's eyes were glued on her. He felt he had incurred her father's disfavor by jiggling the scope, and he hadn't even seen the bird in question.

"You can hardly tell him from the reeds, the way he's holding his head," Heidi commented.

"That's his strategy," her father said. "He blends himself in with the surroundings, holding his beak up in the air so he looks like a reed and can surprise his prey. He would probably like to catch a little water snake or some large beetle among the reeds or possibly a shallow water fish."

Todd stayed close to Heidi as they left the pond and proceeded on through the meadow. He could hear Heidi's father lecturing about finches, larks, and sparrows, but his thoughts were of Heidi and the overwhelming feeling of being in love. He had certainly never been in love before. Last year he had made this play for Janine Anderson and had liked her a lot. But that wasn't really love. He knew it now. He had only wanted to hang out with Janine because his best friends, Steve and Art, were dating two of Janine's friends and it would have made up a good gang. But Janine had been in love with the basketball player, Craig Matthews, and now Todd knew how she had felt. It was really a powerful feeling that put you just about out of action for concentrating on anything besides the person you loved.

The field trip crossed the meadow, and then the pathway led along the edge of steep cliffs along the Pacific Ocean. Looking down, they could see strips of beaches.

"I wonder if you can get down there?" Todd asked.

"Sure. I've been there. Maybe we could go down and eat our lunch," Heidi suggested.

The sun was high in the heavens, and Todd realized lunchtime was approaching. "Gosh, I didn't bring any lunch," he said.

"Of course not," Heidi said, "because you didn't know you were coming. But you can share ours. Dad always brings some extra." She called to her father and asked if they could stop for lunch. He took a vote, and everyone turned out to be hungry.

Heidi got some sandwiches and apples from her dad, and then she showed Todd a ravine in the cliff where they could descend to the beach. Todd hoped that he and Heidi would be the only ones eating lunch there, but the hotshot never missed anything. He spotted them lowering themselves down the rocks and yelled to some others, "Let's go down here with the Princess." On the way down, he kept showing off his knowledge, by pointing out birds' nests in the cliffs.

As they made their way down the embankment, now and then a rock would slip, and Todd had occasion to take Heidi's hand or grab her arm or even put his arm around her waist for support. It was just a natural part of going down a cliff. It just happened. He didn't even have to get up nerve enough to do it, and when they were finally down on the sand, he felt his acquaintance with Heidi had progressed a hundred percent. There were all these college guys and girls hanging around, though. The hotshot, who was a big, burly fellow, once picked up Heidi and ran over to the surf pretending he was going to throw her in and making her scream. But he was only teasing her as though she were a little girl. Todd managed to get Heidi off into a crevice between a couple of rocks, where they ate lunch.

"These college fellows really make up to you," he commented.

Heidi wrinkled her nose and made a wry smile. "They're just trying to get in good with Dad. You know, paying attention to me is kind of like the apple for the teacher. It gets a little tiresome, actually. After all, I'm not a little kid anymore."

Todd viewed her perfect face and privately thought that she was a full-fledged goddess. But he didn't say anything. He just gulped down a bite of tuna fish sandwich. He wished he could grab her and kiss her right then and there, but he wasn't ever going to do that until he was sure it was okay with her. He recalled trying to kiss Janine Anderson after the Homecoming dance last year, and that didn't turn out okay because of Janine's infatuation with the basketball player, Craig Matthews. It might not turn out right with Heidi, either. There was this Joe, who must be a boyfriend of hers. Todd resolved to take it easy and not get in over his depth with his feelings for Heidi—any more than he already was.

After they finished their sandwiches, they ran along the surf a little, and then the college kids got after them to go back up the cliff so the field trip could progress. There was still a lot of ground to cover.

"The beach is my favorite place in the whole

world," Heidi said over her shoulder to Todd as they emerged onto the meadow at the top of the cliff. "I could just be a beachcomber for all my life."

"I like it here, too," Todd agreed. "Something about how far out across the world you can see and the sound of the surf and the smell of the mist. It gives me a real charge."

Heidi reached for his hand to help him up the cliff, her dimples playing around a little smile that seemed to say that she and Todd had a lot in common, and Todd could almost feel his love for her surging and deepening, seeming to expand him.

"Now we come to a place where you can pretend to be Lawrence of Arabia," Heidi said, for the meadow suddenly gave way to a stark scene of sand dunes, striped by the wind into abstract patterns. They ran over the hills and valleys, their feet sinking into the dunes, their footsteps being covered at once by shifting sands. The sky, over the golden dunes, was a startling blue, reflecting in Heidi's eyes to enhance her beauty. The rest of the party trudged along behind them.

"Be careful, now," Dr. Holmstrom admonished. "Any moment, you may encounter a seal, and they can be dangerous." They had come to a ranger station, where Heidi's father presented a card showing he was a biologist who was authorized to enter the elephant seal breeding grounds.

They approached cautiously. In the distance, they could see that the dunes gave way to a beach broken by flat layers of slate-like rock.

"The seals may be partially camouflaged by sand, so you could practically step on one," Dr. Holmstrom warned.

Heidi and Todd encountered a huge seal lying in a protected sunny place behind a dune. It was throwing sand upon its back with its flippers. "Here's one, Dad," Heidi called.

Dr. Holmstrom inspected the seal. It was a female seal, waiting for a seal pup to be born. He told the class that the seal weighed about a ton, and that they would find other female seals nearby and a male seal guarding his harem.

"Watch out for the male seal. He will weigh about two tons and may be very belligerent." Down the beach, there was an increasing number of the huge seals, and Heidi's father pointed out a giant male seal with a wrinkled, ludicrous nose like an elephant's trunk. It was obvious where the animals got their name. They could see another male approaching awkwardly on its flippers along the sand, and the first giant bull seal raised his head in the air, turned back his trunk-like nose, and opened his mouth to give a formidable roar. Todd saw huge, frightening, sharp teeth as the seal bellowed at his rival to keep his distance. Todd felt that he was in some primitive landscape. The elephant seals did not look like inhabitants of the twentieth century. It was as if today he had entered a new world and had become a different person.

Heidi's father told the class that the baby seals would be born in a few weeks and would stay ashore until March, when they had their fur coats and could fish for themselves.

"That old bull is pretty cross because he can't go out and fish. He has to live off his blubber while he guards his family, and he's getting pretty hungry," Dr. Holmstrom added.

"Look through the binoculars to that island over there, and you'll see Sealsville," Heidi told Todd.

Todd trained his glasses on an island a few hundred feet offshore. "It's wall-to-wall seals!" he exclaimed.

After they had seen the seals, they made their way once more across the dunes, around the cliffs, past the lake, and back to their cars. As they rounded the cliffs, they paused to focus their binoculars on an inlet, which was known to be a haunt of the harlequin duck. The hotshot seemed morose that he could not find the rare specimen. Then the group prepared to leave the preserve.

"I wish I could go in the same car with you," Todd whispered to Heidi as they returned.

"Let's just get in Dad's car, and somebody who was in here before will have to go in the car you were in," Heidi said, her deep blue eyes sparkling conspiratorially.

On the way home, sitting so close to her, feeling her warmth, and surrounded by the sound of her voice, Todd's love for her reached the point of no return. They talked about the subjects they took in school, the relative merits of their respective high schools, and about their families. Heidi just had the two little twin brothers, Jackie and Jamie, and Todd told Heidi about Sandy, so that when they arrived at the Holmstroms' home, they knew quite a bit about each other. Todd resolved that he was going to have Heidi for his girlfriend. To be worthy of her, he was going to work for all A's. He was going to be the best president a senior class of his school had ever had, keeping out of trouble, and seeing that none of the other seniors caused trouble.

It was late in the day, and when Todd saw his car sitting in the Holmstroms' drive, he suddenly returned from the dream world he had been inhabiting. He had left the family car here and had not even let his mother or father know where he was! He had been too bewitched by Heidi Holmstrom. He was in for it!

"Do you want to come in for a cold drink?" Heidi asked, "just to rest up before you start home?" Todd now knew that Heidi had started to like him.

"I can't. I've already been away too long. My family doesn't even know where I am," Todd said, with a touch of panic. "And I have to work tonight. I work at this pizza parlor. Only, Heidi"—he looked at the clear oval of her face and into her deep blue eyes—"I wondered if I could call you up sometime—in fact, maybe next Saturday when I have a night off. And we could go to a movie or somewhere."

Heidi looked thoughtful and then gazed into the distance. Did she have a date with Joe, or someone? Then she said, "Well, sure. Why not?" as if the idea of going out on a date with him had not occurred to her before, but now that it did, she found it acceptable.

"Then I'll call you later in the week." His face was suffused with a radiant joy as he drove off toward home. He was practically transformed by his love for Heidi. As he drove, he thought again of what an inspiration she was, and of the good things he was going to do. He would become fast friends with the principal. He would then go to State and learn to be a real hotshot, the first to spot a rare species, in solid with Heidi's father. Then he was going to ask Heidi to marry him and be with her forever. His life was all mapped out, thanks to the wandering habits of Jupiter the peacock.

As Todd pulled up in his driveway, his father thundered out the front door of the house, demanding, "Where have you been all day with that car?" and the rosy bubble of Todd's dream burst, as he emerged into unpleasant reality.

Behind his father, Todd could see the accusing faces of Sandy and his mother.

"I didn't have any way to get to my ballet lesson," Sandy shrilled.

"How did you expect me to do the grocery shopping?" Mrs. Roberts demanded. "And your father had some important business to attend to this afternoon."

"And Steve and Art were over here. Said you had

agreed to meet them and hadn't showed up," his father scolded.

"Gosh, I didn't realize." Todd cringed at the triple onslaught. "I just took those peacocks back where they belonged, and the man who owns them—Dr. Holmstrom—was going out on a field trip to see the elephant seals, and he asked me to go along, and I've never seen the elephant seals, so I went, and I guess I was so excited to go on a trip like that with a real biology teacher that I kind of forgot I had the car."

"You could have called us," his mother scolded.

"One of us could have driven you over and left you," his dad fumed. "You know how much running around in the car we have to do on a Saturday."

"Gosh, Dad, I know. I really didn't mean to. I just didn't think about that when I got this chance to go on the field trip." The image of the enchanting, dimpled Heidi rose briefly in his thoughts and then was erased by the unpleasantness of his father's tirade.

"You need not expect to drive the car for the next month." His father scowled. "Consider yourself grounded."

"Gosh, a whole month?"

"We didn't even know what had happened to you!" his mother added. "We didn't know but that you'd had an accident on the way, wherever you were."

"In Berryville," Todd answered, Heidi's face swimming again through his imagination. "Well, anyway, I'm sorry. I didn't think."

"You can say that again," Sandy said in an out-raged tone. "I had to call Vicky for a ride, and we were late for our lesson. We missed the warming-up exercises and got a bawling out."

"I have to get over to the pizzeria. It's my night to work," Todd mumbled, feeling diminished.

"You better get a move on, because you have to walk. And you'll have to hoof it everywhere for the rest of this month," his dad reminded him.

Todd remembered with a feeling of anguish that he had made a date with Heidi for Saturday night, and now was without wheels.

4

Todd ran upstairs, the whole family following him with outraged eyes. On his dresser, there was a postcard that had come in the mail that day. He picked it up and read the fine writing on the back: "Got your letter, and I'm looking forward to seeing you in a few weeks. We spend a lot of time on the beaches down here. It has been a fantastic experience. Love, Janine." On the other side of the postcard was a long stretch of beach with umbrellas and lots of people. At last Janine had written to him, but only a postcard, compared with the three-page letter Todd had written to her. What a dilemma! She would get back expecting Todd to be in love with her, but now he was in love with someone else. Craig Matthews, Janine's old love, would be away at college, and Janine would be expecting Todd to hang around her; only now that Heidi had come into his life, he wasn't interested. It was going to be an embarrassing situation. And then there was that

Jennifer, who was sort of pursuing him. Life got pretty messy at times.

Todd put on his white coat with the little pizzeria sign on the right pocket and left with his family still glaring at him. As he jogged down to the restaurant, catastrophic thoughts occurred to him. He had told Heidi he would call her about the date. What would he do? He was already tired when he reached the pizzeria and took his chef's hat out of the closet. He must have walked about ten miles today to see the elephant seals.

"There won't be much pizzaz in my pizzas tonight, guys," he told his fellow workers. As he worked with the pizza dough, attempting to look good-natured, he worried about his date with Heidi. Maybe he could double-date with Steve and Sarah. Steve could drive, and he would sit in back with Heidi, which was a pretty good position to be in, if you really loved someone and hoped to kiss her. It was practically impossible when you were driving until you actually stopped at her house, and by that time she was on her guard, and you had to worry about whether her folks were looking out the window.

Somehow, though, Todd didn't want Sarah and Steve to share his first date with Heidi. He and Steve had gotten into so much mischief together that some of it was sure to come up in the conversation. Who knew what stories they would tell Heidi about Todd, and she might get the wrong impression of him, whereas, with her inspiration, he was kind of a new person—a more serious person than the cut-up that Steve and Sarah knew him as. And somehow, he didn't want the people at Blossom Valley High to know about Heidi until he at least knew her better. He wanted her to be his own magical secret, not connected with the drudgery and hassles that people had to go through at school.

In fact, one of those hassles was to take place on

the following Wednesday afternoon—the first meeting of the senior class with himself as president. Through the week, Todd frequently referred to the agenda that he and the principal had made up, and sometimes he stood in front of his bedroom mirror with a fierce, authoritative, presidential look on his face. He got the hammer out of the tool drawer in the kitchen and rapped it on top of the dresser. "The meeting of the senior class is called to order!" he said loudly. That's the way it was done in the movies and on TV.

"Is somebody in there with you?" Sandy stuck her head in the door.

"How many times do I have to tell you to stay out of my room?" Todd glowered.

The meeting of the senior class was to be held in the large classroom where they had the American History class and other large classes that everyone was required to take. Todd went in early. He was worried about whether he could keep order. There must be 250 seniors in the class, and when they all got together, they might get rowdy.

Sarah and Steve also came early. Sarah was the secretary of the class, and she was going to take notes. Todd had already given her the agenda, so she would know what was going to happen. As he waited for the meeting to begin, Todd wished he had never run for president. It was something he did not really think he liked to do. Then Betty Babcock came in. She was not a class officer, but was one of the chief brains of the senior class. Since she had come in so early, she must be an eager beaver, and Todd decided he would appoint her to be in charge of some committee. He reviewed the committees in his thoughts. She would be the one who organized the volunteers. Betty Babcock was a natural organizer. She was very severe looking, with her hair pulled back in a ponytail, and she wore an intense look. If she was in charge of the volunteers, the job would get done. Betty was sort of a General Patton type. She would practically bludgeon people into volunteering, if she was in charge.

Next, Ken Garcia came in. He was the vice-president, who would have to do the job if Todd got sick or was in an accident or anything like that. Art was next, and he had Connie with him. Todd had the uncomfortable feeling that Art would heckle him from the audience and destroy the dignity that he had to maintain while he was president.

A few more people trickled in, mostly girls—Jennifer Baines included. Todd worried that the treasurer had not come yet. He was pretty important. He had to collect money for the parties and graduation invitations and all that. The senior class, in fact, was a more complicated affair than Todd really wanted to be responsible for. But where was everybody? Brett Callaway, the treasurer, finally wandered in, saying he had forgotten what room the meeting was supposed to be held in.

Todd looked apprehensively over the big classroom, where there were only about twenty people. Andy Pearson, the school debating champ, was just coming down the aisle. A few other friends of Todd's came in, people he had especially urged to come to the meeting. It was twenty minutes after the starting time for the meeting.

"We really should get on with it," Betty Babcock said impatiently.

"Everybody isn't here yet," Todd commented. "There's still a couple of hundred people who haven't shown up."

"Probably everybody is here that's coming," Andy Pearson commented. "This is about par for the course."

"Hardly anybody comes to class meetings," Brett

Callaway agreed. He had also been treasurer of the junior class. "Last year, nobody came but the class officers."

"That's right," Betty confirmed. She had been secretary last year. "In fact, this is a pretty good crowd."

"Well, okay," Todd said, recalling that he, himself, had never attended a class meeting. "I guess the meeting is called to order."

"Right on!" Art yelled, and Connie giggled, giving Art a big smile.

Todd told the audience what jobs had to be done, and he appointed Betty the chairman of the school volunteers. Andy Pearson was put in charge of graduation activities, and Jennifer Baines raised her hand and volunteered to run the social events. Todd was a little disgruntled by that, because he had intended to appoint Buzz Wheeler, who played the drums in a combo, to that position. But he didn't want to start a disagreement in the middle of the senior class meeting.

The various committee chairmen chose other people to do jobs, so that eventually everybody at the meeting had something to do: selling graduation invitations or class rings, helping in the library, or something. Jennifer had put Connie in charge of decorating for parties, and Buzz Wheeler was assigned to hire a band for the senior parties. Everything was working out well.

"I vote that we have a big formal Christmas dance," Sarah said, "the very day we get off for the holidays."

"I'm not in favor of that," Todd objected. "There are too many other things going on then. After the holidays, in the rainy season, nobody has anything to do. I vote we have a Valentine dance."

"But Christmas parties are so neat, with a Christmas tree and all," Sarah argued.

"We're all tired from doing tests, and a lot of people go away for the holidays." Todd was determined to have a Valentine dance, and he was going to bring Heidi Holmstrom as his date. Then she, and everybody else, would know he loved her.

"That's right," Connie Caldwell sided with Todd. "Besides, my family is going to Southern California for the holidays, and I won't even be here at Christmas."

When it was put to a vote, the Valentine party Todd had suggested won. They decided that later in the year, near graduation time, they would have a big hamburger and hot-dog barbecue for the seniors. That settled all the business, and Todd adjourned the meeting. Sarah would write up the minutes, and then they would give a copy to the principal, who would see what a good job Todd was doing as president, with responsible people like Betty Babcock and Andy Pearson in charge of committees.

As Todd walked home from the meeting, he wished Heidi could have seen him acting as president. And yet, being president was not such a big deal as Todd had always thought. Only about four people had run for president. It was just a lot of work. Then the chilling thought came to him that he was going to have to do something about that date he had made with Heidi.

Todd fretted all day Thursday. He got Dr. Holmstrom's calling card out of his desk and looked at it and put it back in the drawer. He pounded his fist on the desk top in frustration, thinking how pleasant it would be to call Heidi and confirm the Saturday night date, then to drive over and get her and spend a fabulous evening with her.

He appealed to his father, telling him he had made a date, that after that he wouldn't ask for the car again, but he had to keep the commitments he had already made. Todd's father only smiled a satisfied smile, as if he were almost glad the punishment was inconveniencing Todd.

"No car for a month," he said with finality.

Todd went back upstairs and looked at the phone number again. He tried to work on his biology, but it was impossible. He pictured Heidi sitting out in Berryville, surrounded by peacocks and other exotic birds, anticipating his call, probably wondering what movie they would go to, and deciding what she was going to wear. It could be that Joe had asked her for a date and she had turned him down, saying she had a previous engagement. She was no doubt thinking Todd was a cool, sophisticated guy, and here he would have to call and say his dad wouldn't let him have the car. How puerile that sounded! Would it be better to say that he was sick? That he had some contagious disease and wouldn't want her to get it? That he had been suddenly called out of town on an emergency and wouldn't be back for a month? He ended up not calling her at all on Thursday.

Friday was his last chance. He had to give her at least a day's notice.

"You want to go out and shoot baskets after school?" Steve asked him.

"No, I can't. I have this important phone call I have to make this afternoon."

"A phone call! But that should only take a few minutes."

"It will probably take me a long time to get hold of this person."

"What person is it?" Steve persisted.

"Bug off," Todd said, irritated.

"It must be some girl," Steve deduced. "Who is it? Are you finally turning on to Jennifer? I hope so. Then Sarah will quit heckling me to fix up something with you and her."

"Jennifer Baines it's not."

"So you don't trust me anymore." Steve looked hurt.

"It just happens to be a private matter. I've got to go now," Todd said. He didn't want to alienate Steve, yet Heidi was just someone he wasn't ready to discuss. She was too precious to him to be exposed to the curiosity of others.

Since Todd had to work at the pizzeria that evening, he had only the couple of hours between the end of school and dinner time to make the dreaded phone call. When he got home, Sandy was on the phone. He could hear Sandy giggling to some friend about a boy she liked. Ten minutes later, she was still gossiping and giggling.

"Can't I have any privacy?" she demanded as Todd lurked in the hallway, waiting for her to finish.

"You've been on the phone for hours," Todd complained. "Did it ever occur to you that some-body else might want to use it?"

"I haven't finished yet," Sandy snapped.

Todd fidgeted around in his room for a while, and then checked to find Sandy still talking. He held Dr. Holmstrom's card in his hand, folded it in half nervously, and unfolded it several times, so that it broke in two and had to be taped together. Finally, Todd went out and sat on the stairway right beside where Sandy was phoning. He kept looking at his watch.

Sandy gave him a poisonous glare, but his strategy worked, and soon Sandy slammed down the phone. Todd took it up with trembling hands, the picture of Heidi with her fine light skin and dark blue eyes dominating his thoughts. He mis-dialed the number and then dialed again, concentrating carefully. He hoped Sandy was not listening at the top of the stairs, but he had a hunch she was. He felt his body tense up as someone answered the phone at the other end of the line. It wasn't Heidi, but a lower voice—her mother's.

"Is Heidi there?" Todd asked, an octave above his usual tone.

"No, she won't be here until dinner time. She's practicing. Why don't you call her about six, Joe?"

Joe! Todd's tightly wound-up nerves exploded into a frenzy of alarm. By six, he would be at the pizzeria, and now it was evident that this Joe was a regular caller—the one Heidi's family expected to be calling.

"Okay then," Todd said briefly, not wanting to identify himself. He hung up the phone and a panicky feeling swept over him that he had unpleasant business to finish before a relentlessly approaching deadline. Time was something you couldn't push back; it kept moving up on you like a flood, no matter what important matters had to be settled.

The pizzeria was a busy place on Friday night, and at six o'clock someone was using the phone. On the way over to work, Todd had decided what he was going to say to Heidi. He was just going to tell her the truth of the whole matter. That was the way Heidi was—a person who was open and natural. She wouldn't appreciate some fake story. Another thing Todd thought out on his way there was that Heidi must like him pretty well if she had agreed to a date with him despite having this regular caller, Joe. That was what made the whole thing so agonizing. He had broken in, but now couldn't follow through.

When the customer left the phone booth, Todd hastily put down his pizza dough, wiped the flour off his hands, and made a beeline for the phone. He had the taped-up calling card in his pocket, and when he dialed and heard the phone ringing in the Holmstroms' house, his heart thumped so hard he thought it would flop through his rib cage. Heidi's crisp lilting voice answered, and Todd felt a warm current surge through him on hearing her.

"Heidi, it's Todd Roberts."

"Oh, hi, Todd!" she exclaimed happily. "I've been looking forward to our date tomorrow!"

"Well, that's what I'm calling you about. Something pretty bad has happened."

"Oh?" Todd could feel Heidi's disappointed apprehension through the wires.

"You remember when we went down to see the elephant seals?"

"Of course. It was one of the funnest days I've had."

Todd felt desperate. Did she mean because he was there? He had to see her. "Well, you remember I had my car over at your house." He plunged headlong into his embarrassing predicament. "And I never did tell my folks where I was. So when I got home, they were all furious that I had kept the car out all day, and my dad grounded me for not calling in. So now I can't drive for a whole month, and that means I can't keep our date for tomorrow."

"What a drag! Well, I guess it was our fault, for taking you on the trip. So maybe I could get our car and come over and get you."

"But gosh, Heidi—"Todd's spirits soared at the knowledge that Heidi cared a lot about going out with him—"you would have to drive pretty far by yourself." Somehow it didn't seem right. He should be the one to see her safely home.

"So what? It would be okay. Why should the guys always be the ones to drive? It's a stupid tradition. I'll go ask my Dad if I can. Hold on."

As Todd waited, elation filled him. Heidi was not only beautiful, but resourceful as well. A date with her was going to be a terrific event.

But Heidi's voice was less confident when she

returned. "My dad says he doesn't think it's a good idea for me to drive so far at night when I've had my license for only about three months," Heidi told him. "And besides, he and my mom were planning to go out to dinner in the car tomorrow night, anyway. What he suggested was, why don't we all go out to dinner together? We could come over and pick you up."

Todd had never heard of anything so bizarre. It was kind of like double-dating with Heidi's parents. How weird! What could he say? "Well, do you want to?" he asked cautiously. "Gosh, Heidi, I feel terrible about all this!"

"Why should you?" Heidi asked. "Sure. I want us to go. Why should we both sit at home?"

"Well, if that's what you really want, sure."

"Then we'll pick you up at six-thirty."

Todd felt dazed as he went back to his station in the window to twirl his crusts. As he thought about it, he began to feel pretty good about the whole situation. Heidi wanted to go out with him enough to cook up these plans. And it couldn't hurt him any to get better acquainted with the parents of the girl he loved. Todd pictured them going out to dinner. Dr. and Mrs. Holmstrom would be in the front seat, he and Heidi in back. The Holmstroms would probably be talking about their own affairs, and he might get a chance to kiss Heidi on the way while her parents weren't watching. Of course, if he didn't succeed, it would be pretty embarrassing to have her protesting right in back of her mother and dad. Maybe he could just inch up on her, getting closer and closer until he could tell she was not going to push him away; then, suddenly, they would be kissing.

The next day Todd had to do some pruning around the yard for his dad. As he clipped, he worried about the evening. Would they just honk for him, or would

Heidi come up for him? It was kind of a backward date.

He took a long time getting ready: showering, shaving, slathering some of his dad's after-shave on himself. He was going to wear a plaid blazer and blue slacks. If Heidi had liked him before, she might just go overboard when she saw him in his blazer. But, of course, nothing much would happen anyway, with Heidi's folks along.

Todd was all ready and taking frequent peeks out the window during the fifteen minutes before the Holmstroms arrived. It was Heidi's father who came up to the door after him, and he looked a little surprised to see Todd so dressed up. Dr. Holmstrom was wearing a down jacket and khaki slacks, kind of like he had worn on the field trip. Todd guessed he was one of those casual, rugged guys who never got dressed up.

Out in the darkness, Todd couldn't see Heidi in the backseat at first, and he had a fluttery feeling in his stomach to think of sliding in beside her. But when he opened the car door and the overhead light went on, he saw to his surprise that not only Heidi was in the backseat, but located between him and Heidi were two little car seats, holding Jamie and Jackie.

Heidi cast him an adorable, dimpled smile that made his heart flop over. Each time he saw her, he was astonished again at her freshness and perfection. Yet she looked impossibly inaccessible way over on the other side of the car.

"I don't believe you were properly introduced to my mother," Heidi said. "Mother, this is Todd Roberts."

"I did catch a glimpse of you last Saturday." Heidi's mother smiled around at him. She was a very pretty lady, who looked a lot like Heidi. "And then I've been hearing about you ever since."

"It's a pleasure to meet you, Mrs. Holmstrom," Todd said in his most presidential voice. He wanted to be as poised and at ease as Heidi always was. Besides, his spirits soared to hear that Heidi had been mentioning him.

"And you probably remember my little brothers. Jamie and Jackie, this is Todd."

"Todd, dot," Jamie said.

"Bot, cot, sot," Jackie echoed. They went on with their game, giggling until they were overcome with laughter.

"That's enough, boys. Quiet down," Mrs. Holmstrom scolded.

"Yes, be quiet, Jackie, Jamie," Heidi added, casting a sympathetic glance at Todd. "Todd probably isn't used to silly little kids like you."

"Silly, billy!"

"Willy, hilly!" The twins started another mirthful exchange, going on until they ran out of words. "What's that?" Jackie, who was sitting nearest to Todd, said, pulling Todd's tie out of his blazer.

"Now you leave Todd alone," Heidi admonished. To Todd, she added, "Gee, I'm sorry they're so boisterous tonight."

"It's okay. They're just high-spirited kids with a lot of energy." Todd borrowed a phrase he had heard his father use about himself.

Heidi's father pulled up at a restaurant in a quaint, Hansel-and-Gretel-type building with diamond-shaped glass panes in the windows.

"This is a German restaurant. I hope you like German food," Heidi said.

"Sure, it's great," Todd said. No matter what a hectic evening it was turning out to be, anything was okay as long as he was with Heidi.

The waitress led them to a round table and brought two high chairs for Jackie and Jamie. They put them on opposite sides of the table. Mr. and

Mrs. Holmstrom sat on one side and Heidi and Todd on the other.

"Are your ancestors German?" Todd asked Heidi.

"My mom's are. My dad's Scandinavian. Can't you tell by our name?"

"You haven't been bothered by the peacocks this week?" Dr. Holmstrom smiled at Todd.

"Not this week, but they really weren't much bother," Todd assured him.

"What did you think of the seals?"

"I couldn't believe how many there are."

Dr. Holmstrom told him that the seals had only established the colony a few years ago.

"Do you take your class down to see them every year?"

"Yes. That's one of our standard field trips."

"I might go on it again next year, because I'll probably be going to State."

"Have you applied?"

"Not yet. First I have to take the SAT tests."

Dr. Holmstrom asked Todd what he was taking at school and seemed to be glad he was taking biology. Heidi's mother smiled at him a lot. Todd thought she must approve of him as a friend for Heidi.

Jamie took up a spoon and hurled it across the table onto Todd's plate, where it made a big clatter. Then the Holmstroms stopped talking to Todd and concentrated on getting Jamie to calm down. They gave him a package of crackers, which he broke in little pieces while trying to get the cellophane off.

Heidi put her hand on Todd's arm, as she had done over at his house when the peacocks were there. "I'll bet you're not used to having such little kids at the dinner table," she said.

"It's no problem." Todd smiled at her. "In fact, I was just thinking, I was probably that type of kid when I was their age."

71

"You must have been really cute," Heidi said flirtatiously, "to grow up the way you did."

Todd could feel his face flushing at the unexpected compliment. He was trying to think of something he could say that would let Heidi know in a subtle way how much he loved her, when suddenly he felt a splat and saw that Jackie had stuck his chubby fist in a bowl of applesauce and flung it out toward Todd, splattering one of his lapels and tie.

"We had better move those little rascals over between us," Dr. Holmstrom said, getting up and coming around to move Jackie's high chair. Heidi was leaning over toward Todd with a napkin that she had dampened in her water glass and was wiping the applesauce off his suit. "Oh, and you looked so nice," she said, a tiny frown marring her perfect features. Dr. and Mrs. Holmstrom were fussing around with Jackie's and Jamie's high chairs and were not looking at Todd and Heidi.

"It's okay. It's worth anything to be with you," he said very softly, his eyes caressing hers, and she gave him that twinkly, dimpled smile that told him she liked him a whole lot. Then they just ate their dinners and tried to ignore the twins, while they talked about various things they liked. A couple of times Todd was able to reach over and squeeze Heidi's hand, and they would exchange meaningful looks. It was a good thing they were even able to do that, because Jackie and Jamie were so squirmy in their car seats on the way home that Heidi and Todd each had to take one out and hold them on their laps.

As they neared Todd's house, Dr. Holmstrom invited, "How would you like to go on another field trip with us, Todd?"

"Gee, great. When is it?" Todd asked eagerly.

"Two weeks from today. Be over at the house at eight in the morning," he directed.

"You're going?" Todd asked Heidi, peering over Jackie's silky little towhead.

"Of course. We'll have a blast." Heidi smiled at him. "It will be at the beach again. Shorebirds."

Todd adjusted Jackie back in his car seat as he got out at his house, wishing he could kiss Heidi good night, but determining he would manage it somehow at the field trip.

5

All kinds of people claimed Todd's time at school now that he was president. Todd would never have dreamed of having lunch with Andy Pearson, the champion debater, before; but now Andy was always getting together with him to discuss the relative merits of this or that type of graduation invitation and to plan the program. It was still early in the year, but Andy said it wasn't too early, because they had to get speakers lined up and orders in for the invitations and the printed programs.

"First of all, we have to decide whether we want to have embossed invitations or just printed ones." He showed Todd the two samples.

"The embossed ones," Todd decided. "We're only going to graduate once. We might as well do it with class."

"I agree," Andy said. "Also, I think it would be pretty classy to have the programs printed on a kind of beige paper with sepia letters." He plied Todd with every detail. He was a very organized person, with a special accordion-like portfolio with all his graduation materials in it. Todd decided he would get one for his presidential papers.

"It's also important to get our speakers lined up early," he said, "because some of them will be important civic figures who have heavy commitments—the mayor, for instance."

"The mayor?" Todd croaked. He hadn't planned to be involved with him.

"Of course. We'll invite him to speak. He can follow your address."

"My address?"

"As president of the senior class, you'll have to make a speech. You are noted around school as something of a comic, and I thought you could play that up with something light and humorous, the sort of thing you did in your campaign. The graduating seniors will love that. It will be a good contrast to the mayor, who tends to give a pretty heavy-type speech full of clichés. My own speech comes last, after the superintendent of schools gives his."

Andy went on and on with his details. Sometimes he even phoned Todd at home to ask him about some matter. He wondered if Todd thought Mae Chung would be a good person to put in charge of the programs. She could make a survey of printing costs and plan the format, and she was good at design. After all, Andy couldn't do everything. He was going to be pretty heavily involved in debate this year, even traveling around the country to various meets. Todd wished sometimes that Andy would just carry out these plans without discussing each one with him. Then when he had everything planned, he could just show Todd the finished schedule.

Other people also bugged Todd with their preparations. Jennifer Baines was always calling him or getting him to have a soda with her after school, so they could talk about the arrangements for the

Valentine dance. She had already determined from the principal that they could have the gym that night. Todd had the uncomfortable feeling that Jennifer was expecting to be his date for that event, so he sometimes had to get pretty brusque with her. Jennifer was actually a good-looking girl. She had dark hair that was short, with stylish-looking swooshy waves molding into an attractive cap about her animated face. Last year, she had not had any use for Todd, for she had dated a senior who was on the football team and now had graduated and gone away somewhere; Todd did not want to be that guy's successor, though Jennifer made no secret that she was out to get him. In fact, just as he was about to call Heidi to tell her he had enjoyed the dinner with her family, the phone rang; it was Jennifer, going on endlessly about how much money they were going to need to get red-and-white crepe paper and balloons, how they were going to make this big old-fashioned Valentine box to put in the middle of the gym, and how she and Connie were going to try to get the local merchants to donate favors so everyone could get a present out of the Valentine box.

"Good idea," Todd said impatiently, hoping she would hurry up so he could call Heidi.

When he did call her, they talked for a long time. She apologized for the twins' behavior, and he told her how great it was to know what her family was like. She told him about a physiology project she was doing in school, and Todd told him about amusing things that had happened at the pizzeria.

"I wish I could take you out to that movie we didn't get to go to," he said, "but I guess it will have to wait till my month of penance is over."

"Oh, well," Heidi said. "Anyway, we can go on the field trip the weekend after next."

"This time I'll have my dad bring me over," Todd laughed. "And I'll bring my own lunch."

Todd called Heidi again early the next week, but she was out playing volleyball. Todd kept learning new things about her. Now he found that she was athletic. Later that night he called her up again to tell her how much he looked forward to the field trip. "I heard you were out playing volleyball," he said.

"Yeah, I'm on the school's team. We won today!"

"How could your team fail, with a superstar like you?"

"What a flatterer."

Todd wondered if he was laying it on too thick, and if he should cool it. "Well, I'll see you Saturday," he ended.

"I'm counting the hours," she said. Todd could hardly believe it. She really liked him a whole lot, and she wasn't coy about it. The week dragged on, the longest one Todd had ever known. He daydreamed about Heidi incessantly. In his classes, he had to pull his mind forcibly away from its tendency to concentrate on her. One of the things he had resolved was to get good grades to be worthy of her, but how could he do it if he was preoccupied with thoughts of her? Instead of seeing what the teacher was writing on the blackboard, he was seeing an image of himself and Heidi running hand in hand down the beach, laughing with the happiness of being together. He felt that Saturday would never come.

On Friday afternoon, Steve accosted Todd in the hall. "You want to go over to take the SAT with me tomorrow?" he asked. "My mom is taking me over. We're picking up Sarah, and then we could come by and get you."

"The SAT!" Todd exclaimed, thunderstruck. "Tomorrow! That's not when it is! I'm going on this field trip tomorrow."

"On the day of the SAT? You got your notice, didn't you? You said you signed up for it."

"Well, I did, but tomorrow! Are you sure?"

"Sure I'm sure. I've been dreading it all month, hating the thought. Now, I'm only glad the time is almost here, and I'll get it over with."

Disaster had overtaken Todd again. He had goofed, and it was going to affect his relationship with Heidi. With a stricken look, he told Steve, "I'll call you tonight if I need a ride."

Todd hurried home and looked in his desk drawer through a rumple of papers. If only he could be as well organized as Andy Pearson, at once he would have found his notification that he was to take the test. He had even paid quite a lot to take it. Without that score, he couldn't get in college. At last he found the notice. As Steve had said, the test really was tomorrow. It was to be given in some room in the junior college. It took up practically the whole day. Just about all the seniors would be there. How could he have forgotten? What did he do now about Heidi? For the second time, he had arranged to meet her and had to call and cancel the plans. This time, he didn't think he could do it. He would just not show up.

No, that wouldn't do. He could imagine them all waiting for him and Heidi's disappointment and disillusionment when he didn't come. Putting it off would be to prolong his agony, so about dinner time, he dialed her number, which he now knew by heart. When she answered, he felt that he couldn't breathe or talk.

"Heidi?" he said fearfully.

"Yes?" There was a question in her voice in response to his uncertain tone.

"This is Todd."

"I know," she said playfully. "Don't you think I recognize your voice by now? Is something the matter?"

"Everything is the matter."

"What's wrong? Has something happened to you?"

"Something really bad."

"What is it?"

Todd hesitated a long time.

"Well, what's the matter, Todd?" There was an edge of alarm to her voice, and he didn't want to frighten her.

"I can't go on the field trip tomorrow."

"Can't go! But you planned to a long time ago." Heidi's lighthearted tone gave way to an uncharacteristic coldness.

"I just discovered that's the day I have to take the SAT test."

"Well, didn't you know before this?"

"I sort of forgot about it because I wanted to go on the field trip so much."

"I guess if you can't go, there's nothing to be done about it." Heidi sounded really miffed and put off by the news. In fact, she sounded disgusted with him. She was finding that he was a bungler who couldn't keep his life in order, and she must be revising her opinion of him.

"Heidi," Todd said desperately. "I'll be able to get the car again soon. Maybe just you and I can go down and see the shorebirds some time."

"Maybe," she said crisply. "But I have to go now. I was just setting the table, and my mom is anxious to get dinner on." Todd thought he heard something like a kind of sob in her voice, but he couldn't be sure. He was too agitated himself.

"Well, I'll call you again later."

"So long, then," Heidi said hurriedly, and she hung up. She was really turned off. It wasn't the way she usually talked at all. Everything was spoiled.

The whole thing, Todd felt, affected his performance on the SAT. How could he think, when this test had wrecked his relationship with Heidi? It would be so easy, in the mood he was in, to fill in the wrong section with his number 2 pencil, flunk the test, and not get into State at all—never take courses from Heidi's father. Heidi was probably through with him before they had really begun anything. He had made two dates with her and had had to break them both. He looked at the next question. Somewhere, he had read about the SAT that when you were in doubt, you should not fill in a, c, or e. Life was pretty ridiculous, anyway. All that this test would tell about him would be revealed by a few marks from the number 2, and yet maybe it had ruined his whole life. Because of it, he would probably never marry Heidi or even go to college.

Todd felt pretty low when he got out of the SAT. As he drove home with Steve and Sarah, he thought of Heidi, surrounded by college boys and sandpipers, probably being thrown into the surf by the hotshot. Heidi was sixteen, not too young, really, for one of those college boys to get serious about her. It was bound to happen, when she was so cute and they were all trying to make up to the professor.

"Well, how'd you do?" Steve asked him.

"Lousy." Todd's voice was morose.

"Me, too," said Steve. "I did really badly on the math."

"The math was a real disaster," Sarah agreed. "We'll just have to wait and see what our fate is." Sarah and Steve had decided they both would like to go to UCLA. They were both going to apply to the same schools, and whichever one accepted them both, that's where they would go.

Another week went by, full of urgent senior-class business. It was imperative to order the caps and gowns for graduation now, Andy Pearson told him. Jennifer had lunch with him to tell him that Connie had six people on the decorating committee for the

Valentine party, and that various merchants were donating small heart-shaped boxes of candy, red camellia corsages, romantic books, and cologne for both guys and girls. Jennifer and her committee were going to wrap all the favors for girls in white paper with red ribbons and for the guys in red paper with white ribbons.

"You're doing a great job, Jennifer," Todd complimented her, feeling a little guilty that he couldn't show her the attention she was obviously fishing for. "This may be the best party Blossom Valley High has ever had."

Jennifer cast Todd an alluring look. "Did you remember my New Year's Eve party? It will be here before you know it."

"Oh, sure, I have it down on my calendar." Jennifer fluttered her eyelashes coquettishly. Todd was hoping he wasn't supposed to be Jennifer's partner.

Todd even had lunch with Betty Babcock occasionally. Betty had all the volunteers lined up. "There's better discipline in the cafeteria than there has ever been," Betty told him. "All the teachers have commented to me that their job has been really lightened since you've been president."

"Hey, Betty!" Todd objected. "That's not it. It's since you got to be head of the volunteers."

"But you appointed me," Betty assured him. She seemed to approve of his presidency. Since Betty was one of the great brains of the senior class, Todd took it as a real compliment. Last year, he never would have imagined becoming such good friends with really serious people like Betty and Andy Pearson. Yet this year, he was in thick with them.

It had changed his life to be president. Of course, he had sought the office mainly as a means of getting Janine Anderson to like him. And now he no longer cared whether she did or not. But it enriched him to have developed close relationships with people such as Betty and Andy and Ken Garcia and the other officers—to have enlarged his social circle, which previously had consisted pretty exclusively of his old mischievous friends, Steve and Art.

Todd sometimes wondered how he could keep up his responsibilities as senior class president, his studies, and his work at the pizzeria. On the Friday night a week after the SAT test, he dutifully donned his chef's hat and dug into a big wad of pizza dough, going into his act for the evening.

About ten o'clock, just after the first movie, a whole bunch of kids came in for refreshments, lots of people Todd knew from Blossom Valley High. But in one of the booths, he was electrified to see a group of strangers—and in their midst was Heidi Holmstrom. She knew he worked here. Had she come here on purpose to show him up for breaking his date with her? She was sitting by a big dark-haired guy. Todd found excuses to go by the booth a couple of times. He heard someone addressing the boy next to Heidi as "Joe."

"Oh, hi, Todd," Heidi said offhandedly as he passed by the booth. "I wondered if this was the pizza parlor where you worked."

The other girls in the group looked at him kind of slyly, and the one called Joe gave him a curious and arrogant look. Todd scrutinized the whole group with intense interest. These must be Heidi's best friends. They looked pretty nice. Joe, however, seemed a bit domineering. Heidi quickly introduced Todd around the table as someone she had met on one of her dad's field trips. He couldn't remember any of their names except Joe's. Todd excused himself then, because it was too painful to be around Heidi and yet not be with her. He could see that everyone at her table thought she was fun to be with. They were all laughing and cutting up, but Joe gave him a kind of glower. As Todd started to leave, Joe seemed to be emphasizing Todd's role as a waiter: "Hey," he said, "how about making our pizza with extra pepperoni?"

Todd just put up his hand with the thumb and forefinger shaped together into an "O," then went behind the counter and told the other guys to fix the pizzas for Heidi's table with lots of extra everything. He looked over to the booth and saw that Heidi was watching him, grinned at her, and went back to making the crusts, trying not to look again. She looked too beautiful, and it hurt to think of how he had goofed everything up with her.

Now and then Todd glanced toward their booth. They were eating now, and Joe looked up once and glared at him in a hostile manner. Todd felt uncomfortable about Joe. Naturally, anyone as attractive as Heidi would have a boyfriend, or even several. He had the feeling that Joe looked on him as a rival.

And then Heidi and her friends drifted away, Heidi with a casual little wave to him. Todd was plunged into gloom at seeing Heidi out with the other boy. He puzzled over Heidi's appearance here. He didn't think she had come just to show him up, after he had broken their date. Todd didn't think that was Heidi's style. She was too straightforward. Maybe she just wanted to remind him of her existence. He would find out. He decided to call her to make another date with her after he had his wheels back.

In fact, Todd decided he would invite her to the New Year's Eve party. Jennifer Baines had invited him and a lot of other guys. The others would bring dates. Why shouldn't Todd? He suspected that Jennifer meant him to be her date, but if he invited Heidi early enough and let Jennifer know he had a date, then Jennifer would have to ask someone else as her partner.

The holidays were rapidly approaching. Todd knew he would have to invite Heidi right away to beat Joe to the draw. When he called her the next week, he put on a kind of a clown act, like he used to do, speaking in a thick Italian accent.

"This is the pizzeria calling," he said, "to ask if the pizza you ate at our establishment was satisfactory."

Heidi laughed at his accent, assuring him it was the most super pizza she had ever tasted.

Todd switched back to his own voice, and spoke seriously. "It was kind of painful to see you with another guy." Todd wasn't sure he had a right to say that, since he really hadn't known Heidi very long.

"Joe?" Heidi said in surprise. "He is just somebody I've known since kindergarten."

"That's too long," Todd said. "You need a change. How about going to a New Year's Eve party with yours truly?"

"Oh, Todd!" Todd could hear the excitement in her voice. "I would love to, but I'm going down to Baja with my dad on this bird trip. We're leaving on the fifteenth of December, and we won't be back until January third."

"What a bummer! For me, that is," Todd complained. "Heidi, you're not mad at me that I didn't make the field trip? The SAT is a really important test."

"I know it," Heidi said. "Todd, I'm sorry for being so childish. I was so disappointed when you couldn't come, and I'm afraid it showed. I wish you had been on the trip. Dad said there had never been so many shorebirds as this year . . . and . . . I missed you."

"Heidi, the Saturday after you come back from Baja, could you and I—just we alone—go down to the beach? You could show me the birds. We could go down to Pescadero or one of those other beaches between Half Moon Bay and Santa Cruz."

"Okay," Heidi said with audible delight. "It's a date. But don't you back out this time. Check your calendar, and see if there's anything else going on that day. *And,* ask your dad in advance if you can get the car."

"Right, Heidi. Don't worry, nothing will interfere this time. I've learned my lesson."

"Todd"—Heidi's voice hesitated—"I really wish I could go to the New Year's party with you."

"I wish you could, too. More than you can imagine."

"Well, Merry Christmas, Todd."

"Heidi. Gosh, I can hardly wait for you to get back." Todd's voice revealed his excitement, and Heidi laughed melodiously. "Well, I haven't even gone yet." Todd knew this date was one that was going to work out. They both were anxious to see each other.

As for New Year's Eve, Todd was committed to go, but he didn't want to ask any other girl. Jennifer Baines kept throwing out hints that she expected him to be her partner. In fact, Todd decided that was a pretty safe state of affairs. Jennifer would be busy being the hostess, and he wouldn't have to pay too much attention to her. He would just go, be there, and leave. It was the first New Year's Eve party he had ever been to, except ones his parents had given. It would be a major event.

"Just imagine!" Sarah said as a bunch of the seniors sat around at lunch. "We are going to see Janine again. We'll hear all about South America."

Todd wished he had not written Janine that mushy letter. It made him uneasy. How would he act toward her? He had even written in her school yearbook last year, after he had won the campaign for senior class president, "Next year, I'm campaigning to get you for my girlfriend."

"Craig Matthews will be coming to my New Year's party," Jennifer said. "I phoned his house, and his mother said she would get in touch with him and let me know. So she phoned me back. She said that Craig was taking Janine to another party with some of his old basketball cronies, and then he and Janine would come by my party after going to the other one."

On New Year's Eve, Todd was all tensed up. The party didn't start until nine o'clock, and it was a long time from dinner until then with nothing to do. To make matters worse, Sandy had some of her friends over for a New Year's Eve slumber party. They kept running downstairs to phone people and wish them a Happy New Year. Todd went down to make himself a peanut butter and jelly sandwich to tide him over until it was time for the party, and he found Vicky and Deedee in the kitchen getting soft drinks. They were everywhere. He would be glad to get out of the house.

Over at Jennifer's, it wasn't much better. Janine was supposed to be the guest of honor at the party, and everyone seemed in a state of suspended animation waiting for her and Craig to arrive. Todd milled around eating peanuts and chips and dip and drinking sodas. He must have had six.

"Look what I got for the big midnight scene." Art's eyes were mischievous. He showed Todd a bag of firecrackers behind the kitchen door. Art's dad was a Navy pilot and went to places across the Pacific, where he had bought the unusual firecrackers. Todd's eyes lighted up. "You can help me shoot them off," Art promised.

"Why don't we all dance?" Jennifer flushed the

boys out of the kitchen, and she appropriated Todd as her partner to dance to some loud rock. Todd liked to dance, and he did a lot of clowning as he did so. Then there was a trade of partners, and he found himself dancing with Sarah.

"I wonder when they'll get here," Sarah said impatiently.

"Probably before midnight," Todd said. "Craig Matthews has so many other friends to catch up with. After all, he was the Athlete of the Year." Todd was becoming more and more nervous as he waited for them to arrive. He wished he could have had Heidi as his date, to show Craig and Janine they didn't have to worry about his pursuing Janine anymore.

It was almost 11:30 P.M. when Craig and Janine finally arrived. The doorbell rang, and everyone converged in the front hallway. There was a lot of yelling, and everyone was trying to hug Janine, who was wearing a brightly embroidered dress from Uruguay. Craig beamed broadly with his big charismatic grin. There still was nobody at Blossom Valley High to touch him. He was wearing a short close-fitting black jacket with multicolored flowers embroidered down the front.

"This was Janine's Christmas present to me," Craig told everyone. "It's a gaucho jacket from Uruguay. I thought New Year's Eve was about the only occasion festive enough to wear it." People were throwing serpentine and confetti at Craig and Janine, so they had festoons of paper hanging all over them, and their hair was dotted with confetti.

"The Uruguayan cowboys wear these coats at festivals," Janine added. She looked radiant. When everyone finished hugging her, Craig held his arm loosely about her as if to protect her from the crowd, and he kept looking down at her as if nothing had ever made him so glad as to have her back after her six months' absence.

Todd felt a lump in his throat to see them loving each other so much, and he wished again that Heidi could have come with him. She was just being wasted on a lot of pelicans down in Baja California on New Year's Eve.

6

Craig and Janine moved out of the hallway into the Baineses' living room. They were both wearing gold New Year's hats with red feathers on them from the other party.

"Tell us all about how it was," Jennifer said to Janine.

"It was great. But I've been telling all the guys at the other party about it, and besides, I have to make a speech in an assembly about it when school starts. You would have to hear it twice. So why don't you just tell me about what's been going on at school? I don't know much about what's happened since I left." Suddenly she saw Todd.

"Todd Roberts!" she exclaimed, going over to him. "I can't believe it! What has happened to you? You must have grown ten inches!" She turned to Craig. "Can you believe how Todd has changed?"

"Hey, you really shot up!" Craig agreed. "What

have you been doing? Eating spinach or something?"

"Been stretching myself out too much catching those pizzas," Todd returned, as he had said many times when people commented on his sudden growth.

Janine hooked one arm through Todd's and the other through Craig's. "Let's get caught up," she said. They all sat on a sofa.

"Last time we saw you, you had just gotten elected president," Craig recalled.

"It's no big deal," Todd answered. "I'm surprised you would remember that, after you've been to college and all. How is college, anyway?"

"It's okay," Craig said. "Only I'll be glad when Janine gets over there." He gave Janine an affectionate smile.

"How do you know I'll get in? There's a lot of competition," Janine said, returning his smile with an adoring glance. Todd felt a little uncomfortable to be with people who were so in love.

Jennifer was passing out hats, horns, and noisemakers. "It's almost midnight," she said. "Everybody get ready for the countdown."

As Todd took a hat from her, Jennifer gave him an intimate smile, and Todd recalled with panic that at midnight on New Year's Eve, everybody kisses someone. Craig would kiss Janine, Steve would kiss Sarah, Art would kiss Connie, the others would all be kissing their dates. There would be himself and Jennifer left over. Todd looked for an escape route. He got up from the sofa, put on his New Year's hat, which was like a toy soldier's, with a big paper plume on top, and told Janine and Craig: "I have something to do at midnight. I'll see you later.

"Hey, Art," he said, "aren't you and I going to shoot off the fireworks at midnight?"

"Sure," Art said. "Hey, Connie, you want to

shoot them with us? We're going out in the back-yard. We'll shake up the neighborhood. Let them know a new year has arrived."

"It's pretty cold out there."

"Get your coat, then." Connie looked rather petulant and put out, and she did not make a move to come with them. Art was very excited about the firecrackers. He and Todd ran out into the backyard, and as soon as they heard the bell in the church tower a few blocks down sound the first note of twelve, they put a big firecracker under a metal garbage can and it made an impressive boom. Inside, people blew horns. Art and Todd could hear other people around the neighborhood yelling, ringing bells, banging on pans, and there were a few other firecrackers going off. A string of ladyfingers crackled from a nearby yard.

"Probably got them in Chinatown," Art said, impatient to light the next fuse. Todd threw out a firecracker and blew on a horn at the same time it went off.

It was dark out in the yard, but Todd and Art could see by the light that streamed out of the Baineses' windows. You could see into the living room. Craig and Janine were still seated on the sofa. Craig had his arms around her, and they were deep into a New Year's kiss that looked as if it would never stop. Todd remembered when he had tried to kiss Janine after the Homecoming dance and hadn't succeeded, because she loved Craig so much. Craig and Janine looked like they were practically welded together. He also noticed that Steve was kissing Sarah, and other people also were kissing their friends and yelling "Happy New Year" and twirling noisemakers, blasting horns, throwing confetti, and blowing out the gizmos that rolled out and had little feathers on the end. Craig and Janine didn't seem to notice that any of that noise and activity were going on. They were just lost in each other's arms, in an endless kiss. They deserved some privacy after being apart for six months. Todd looked away. If Heidi had been there, he could have felt like Craig and Janine did, unable to let her go. He longed for her. A big wave of love jolted over him, and he remembered with a little thrill of anticipation that he had a date with her for the next Saturday. He would be with her down on the beach all day. He hoped that he and Heidi would love each other the way Craig and Janine did.

He and Art shot off the rest of the fireworks in rapid succession and added their voices to those that were yelling "Happy New Year" all around the neighborhood. The noise and shouting started to dwindle away then, and Todd felt it was safe to go in. The kissing seemed to be over. Even Craig and Janine had parted, and there wasn't any danger now of Todd getting entangled with Jennifer. In fact, he felt a little guilty, because Jennifer seemed to consider him her date, yet he hadn't paid much attention to her.

"Hey, what happened to Connie? She never came out," Art asked.

"Guess it was too cold," Todd said.

"We better clean this up." Art was picking up debris, and Todd joined him. Then they went in, smelling a little of sulfur. Connie and Jennifer looked at them with some hostility as they entered.

"Hey, how did you guys like that big one?" Todd grinned. "We really welcomed in the New Year right!"

Jennifer looked at him coldly, and Connie was also giving Art the cold shoulder. Art, seeing he was in the doghouse, began to wheedle Connie. "What happened to you, anyway? We thought you were coming out."

"Midnight on New Year's Eve is a very special time," Connie said accusingly. Jennifer was looking daggers at Todd. Todd uneasily remembered that he had to depend upon Jennifer to run the senior class social events, and he had better not arouse her enmity.

"Hey, Jennifer, I never did wish you a happy New Year," he said. He gave her a little perfunctory hug and a faint peck on the cheek. "Art and I were too busy putting your party on the map!"

"Thanks," Jennifer said with somewhat bored irony.

"How about some more dancing?" Todd said, anxious to get back in her good graces. He was a good dancer, if he did say so himself.

"Okay," Jennifer agreed, "and then we're going to have a breakfast."

"I can help. I'm a professional chef, you know," Todd said. He was very attentive to Jennifer for the rest of the evening.

Janine showed everyone a Uruguayan dance called the *Pericón*. "It's a dance the cowboys—called the gauchos down there—do at festivals," she said. "They would be dressed in outfits like Craig has on." Everybody learned the *Pericón*, and then they had a breakfast of scrambled eggs, ham and sausages, Danish, and the works.

While they were eating breakfast, they persuaded Janine to tell them more about Uruguay. "I'll bet you were pretty conspicuous among the Latinos with your blonde hair," Ken Garcia commented.

"Not really," Janine said. "There are lots of blondes in Uruguay. The country was settled by a lot of Middle Europeans, not just people from Spain and Portugal. And strangely enough, there were no native Indians in that part of South America. Uruguay is known as the 'Switzerland of South America'—mostly because it's a kind of banking and financial center. But I'm not going to go into a long discussion about the country, because then you'll all be bored hearing it again in the assembly."

"Besides, she still has jet lag," Craig said, looking down at her protectively.

"How's the basketball going?" Todd asked Craig.

"We've had a couple of practice games, and the season opens officially next Friday," Craig said. "Hey, that's right, you're a basketball aficionado. How would you like a couple of free tickets to the game next Friday?"

"It's pretty far over to Berkeley," Todd said, "but maybe I could. I would sure like to see a college game. In fact, my dad and mom are going to some convention from Friday to Monday, and my aunt is coming to stay over at our house, so I get the car all weekend."

"Well, hey, why don't you come over then?" Craig produced the two tickets from his wallet, and then he took Todd aside with a confidential air.

"Hey, Roberts," he said. "I just got a really great idea. You and Janine have always been such good friends, and I know Janine wants to see one of the games. I was wondering if you could bring her over with you. After the game, I'll take you guys out on the town. Show you all the college dives."

"Wow!" Todd said. "That would be super." Todd imagined what a memorable evening it would be to hang out with a star basketball player at a big college, and then to go out with such a celebrity after the game. But Todd felt a little funny taking a girl out for a date with another guy.

Craig's face wore a kind of serious frown. "It's going to be pretty hard for Janine and me to see each other, because basketball takes up so much of my weekend. So it would really be a favor to me if you would bring her over. I'll even pay for the gas, 'cause it's a pretty long trip."

"Oh, you wouldn't need to, but it might help, because I also have to drive down to the beach on Saturday," Todd said. He wondered what Craig would think if he knew about the letter he had written Janine—how he had plotted to get Janine away from Craig.

"Let's talk it over with Janine." Craig pulled Todd's arm, and they went back to Janine. Todd had a fleeting feeling of reluctance. He was in a strange position. If it had been anyone except Craig Matthews who had asked him, he would have felt he was being used. But both Janine and Craig were really great people. He knew how they felt about each other, and he really wanted to go.

Craig's face lit up with his wonderful grin when he saw Janine. "Guess what?" he told her. "Roberts just happens to be going over to the game at Berkeley next Friday, and he says he wouldn't mind having an extra passenger. Afterward, we'll go out and hit the night spots."

Janine gave Todd a radiant smile. "Really? Oh, how terrific!"

Todd gulped. This was not something he would have cooked up himself. He was very surprised, in fact, to find himself booked up for the long drive to get Janine and Craig together that evening. He got into the weirdest situations! A guy with Craig's charisma could talk anybody into anything. "You're sure we're not imposing on you?" She looked searchingly at Todd.

"Gosh, no," he assured her. "It will be a blast to go check out the big college town on Friday night and see all the action."

Todd telephoned Heidi to make sure she was back from Baja California and to verify their date before he went to pick up Janine the next Friday. He was a little distracted when he met Janine, and kind of wished he were not going over to Berkeley, but could just stay home and rest up for tomorrow and dream about Heidi. His preoccupation must have gotten through to Janine, because she said, "This is a pretty long drive for you to make, just for a basketball game. Craig shouldn't have asked you to do it."

Todd felt uncomfortable. He was afraid Janine still thought he was romantically interested in her, and he wanted to be as casual as possible. "No, I really wanted to go," he assured her. "I get tired of doing the same old stuff every Friday night—going to lousy movies, raising cain with Steve and Art. There are a lot more interesting things to do when you get to college."

"Next year, we'll be there," Janine said. "I'm getting my application for Berkeley ready."

"I'm not going over there," Todd told her. "I'm going down to State. Hey, tell me more about South America. What was it like—the town where you lived?"

"Montevideo? It was a picturesque city. Very old. There was a hill near it, 'El Cerro,' which they called a mountain. The city is on a river, the Rio de la Plata, which in most places you can't see across, where it flows into the Atlantic Ocean. One day we went on a boat trip across it, and we ended up in Buenos Aires, Argentina. So I got to see another country. Buenos Aires is a really big, fancy city." Janine went on chattering about the family she had lived with, and her friend, Esperanza.

"The bad part about going to live in another country is that you get so involved in the life, and you make friends, and just as you start to feel like you belong, you have to leave. Even though I wanted to get back here, I felt wrenched away, as though I had a lot of unfinished business."

"Did you have any boyfriends down there?" Todd teased.

"The Uruguayans are very strict about boyfriends.

Esperanza went to a Catholic girls' school, and so I went with her. It was very strange. We weren't even allowed to see any boys without being chaperoned. I feel funny right now to be going all this distance with you. The Urrutias would be scandalized. I used to tell Esperanza how we went out on dates, and she couldn't believe it. She is dying to come and visit me and see if it's true."

"Weird!"

"You want to hear what the Spanish sounds like down there? A lot different from the way we learn it." Janine launched into some rapid, heavily slurred Spanish.

Todd whistled. "Wow! You are really fluent. I can't even understand you, even though we used to be in the same Spanish class last year. Anyway, I'm not even taking Spanish now because I decided to go in for biology and chemistry and all that." Todd thought maybe he should tell Janine about being in love with Heidi, but they were already coming into Berkeley. Craig had given Janine directions for getting to the basketball pavilion, and she had written them down. So while Janine was directing Todd, he didn't have a chance to tell her he had this new girlfriend.

"Turn left here," Janine directed, and soon they were in the parking lot, and then they found the entrance to the pavilion and got into their seats.

"It seems funny not to know anybody at a basketball game," Todd remarked, looking around at a sea of strangers.

"Yeah," Janine agreed. "It's not like last year. Remember when we used to go to the games, and you would throw paper wads at all your friends and horse around?"

"I've kind of outgrown that."

"You sure have changed a lot, Todd. More than anybody else I have seen."

"After all, it's been six months since you've been gone, and a lot of things have happened since then."

"You have all the responsibility of being president."

"Yeah, and . . ." Todd was about to tell her about his new girlfriend, but the whistle blew and the game began.

"Where is Craig?" Janine searched among the players that had just run out on the floor.

"Gosh, I don't see him," Todd said. "That *is* the Cal team, isn't it? The ones in the red trunks?"

"Yeah, it's them. They are so *big!* And I can't find Craig."

The players moved out onto the floor, jumping, dribbling, running, passing, a jumble of arms and legs shifting rapidly around the court. Todd and Janine were confused. These weren't the old, familiar faces of the well-known high school teams whose relative standings Todd knew. Then Todd saw Craig. He was standing up by the players' bench grinning at them and trying to catch Janine's attention.

"Hey, Janine. There's Craig." Todd pointed him out.

"But he's not playing." Janine looked disappointed.

"He just didn't start. He'll be in later."

The game went on. They could hear the thump of the ball against the backboard, the sound of running feet, the referee's whistle, the yells of the crowd. Once Todd saw Janine yawn. She put up her hand, embarrassed. "I'm still operating on Montevideo time," she explained. "It's hard to get adjusted."

Now and then, Craig would look up at them and smile. The Cal team was losing.

"If they would only put Craig in, they would probably win," Janine complained. "They were so anxious to get him over here, and now they won't even let him play."

"You have to remember, he's only a freshman," Todd replied. "I can hardly wait for the game to be over, so we can go out and see those dives Craig was telling us about."

"Me, too," Janine said. "After all, this might be my home for a while."

Todd and Janine went down to wait for Craig at the gate he had specified. They didn't have to wait long. He sneaked up from behind Janine and put his arms around her, startling a scream out of her, and then he gave her a playful kiss and put his hand out to shake Todd's.

"I see you found the place okay." He smiled. "We'll get an early start. Since I didn't play, I didn't even have to shower. The first thing on the agenda is food. There's a good Italian place."

"Pizzas are out," Todd warned. "Remember, I work at a pizzeria."

"Oh, right," Craig laughed, putting his arm around Janine. "We'll try someplace else. We have to eat at three-thirty in the afternoon before a game, and by the time the game is over we're ravenous again." They walked down the street, and Craig pointed out a Chinese restaurant. "This one is supposed to be good. I've never tried it, though."

"I'm a Chinese food freak," Todd admitted. "And you never go out of a Chinese restaurant hungry."

As they crunched wontons and prawns and tried out chopsticks on slippery bean sprouts and elusive pieces of chicken and cashews, Craig told them about life at college. "I'll show you my room after dinner," he promised. "Since I have this basketball scholarship, I live with the other players. All of us have to study really hard. There's tough competition here, a lot of real brains. And if we don't make good grades, it's no more basketball."

They cracked open their fortune cookies. Craig's said: "Your best asset is your sunny smile."

"That's correct," Janine said, opening hers. "You are lucky in love," she read, snuggling up to Craig.

"It's always darkest before the dawn," Todd read. "What's that supposed to mean? That I'm in for some bad luck?"

Craig showed them his dorm, where his roommate, a super-tall black guy, was getting ready to go out for dinner. "He didn't get to play, either," Craig told them. "He's got a pulled hamstring."

Craig showed them around the campus, taking them to the main square by the student union, where there were students milling about. They ended up at a tiny restaurant that served dessert and cappuccino. Over the coffee, Janine complained, "How come they didn't let you play?"

Craig laughed his easy laugh. "Maybe if we had been winning, they might have let me in for a few minutes. Face it, honey, I'm not the star over here."

Janine and Todd looked around. Nobody seemed to know Craig. Over at Blossom Valley High, everything had pretty much come to a stop when he appeared.

"I've got to be getting back," Todd said, finally. "I've got to get up early. I have this date to go to the beach."

"I'm kind of tired, too," Janine said. "When will you get back over our way?"

"It's going to be hard, with games every weekend," Craig said. "But I'll phone you."

"You oughta arrange to get over to the senior class Valentine party," Todd urged. "It will probably be the best party the school has ever had. We have this awesome combo lined up, the Dream Weavers."

"Maybe you won't have a game that night," Janine said hopefully to Craig.

"Sometimes we play on Friday and then we have Saturday off. I'll check the schedule," Craig said. "If that happens, reserve a ticket for me. I'll phone and

100

let you know." They were walking toward the parking lot, and Janine and Craig were holding hands. Todd felt left out. He felt even more so when Craig kissed Janine good night before she got into the car. Todd pretended not to be watching, but he really was taking it in, out of the corner of his eye. Up to now, Todd had been such a clown and show-off that no girls had taken him seriously. When he had tried to kiss Janine after the Homecoming dance last year, she wouldn't let him, because she had already fallen so hard for Craig. This year, he would probably have been able to kiss any of quite a few girls, but he wasn't interested in any of them except Heidi. Heidi loomed up in his thoughts as he sat in the car waiting for Janine and Craig to finish. He was impatient to get home and rest up for tomorrow. At last, Janine and Craig tore themselves apart, and Craig opened the car door for Janine and came around to Todd's side of the car to thank him effusively for bringing Janine over. "You don't know what it means to me," he said.

Todd grinned a wide, knowing grin. "I can pretty well guess," he said.

"Thanks again. And good night, Janine. I'll call you next week."

They drove off, leaving Craig waving in the parking lot, looking lonely and abandoned.

It was many miles from Berkeley back down the San Francisco peninsula to Janine's and Todd's homes. They had to go across the long Bay Bridge, which cut through Treasure Island, and then they could see the San Francisco skyline against the night sky, twinkling with the lights from its many tall office buildings. Todd had to concentrate on the heavy traffic, switching lanes to hit the southbound Bayshore Highway. He didn't talk to Janine while he was maneuvering his way from the right side of the freeway to the left.

"Whew!" he said, once he was on the turnoff leading him toward home. "This traffic is a jungle. It would be easy to wreck my dad's car in there."

"Gee, Todd," Janine said. "I know what a drag it has been for you to bring me over. It wasn't really fair to you."

The letter Todd had written to Janine and his last year's crush on her hung awkwardly in the air between them.

"It wasn't a drag. I had fun. A free meal, a look at one of the most fantastic campuses in the country."

"I felt the same way," Janine said. "You know, Todd, I'm kind of worried about Craig. Doesn't he seem different to you? Kind of deflated, or something?"

Todd became wary. He hoped that Janine was not going to get tired of Craig and decide she wanted Todd for a boyfriend. After all, she had that pleading letter Todd had written to her in Uruguay, practically handing his heart over to her. But that had been a mistake, caused by a lonely summer. And that had been before Heidi.

"I guess you get that impression because he used to be such a superstar at Blossom Valley High. Everybody knew him. He was the best athlete and the best-looking and most popular guy. And over there at Berkeley, there are thousands and thousands of people—thirty or forty thousand students, maybe. And they are all pretty good at something. There are hundreds of handsome guys. So now he is kind of a small fry, sitting on the bench and swallowed up in the crowd."

"That's it," Janine said in a subdued voice. "All those other basketball players are older and better than he is, and nobody at the restaurants or around the campus seems to know him."

"Yeah, going away to college can mean going from top dog to one of the mob."

"A little fish in a big pond," Janine echoed sadly.

They were silent for a while. "That's the way I remember it was when we came out of the eighth grade into high school. Everybody looked so big. I felt like a really insignificant runt."

"Yeah, it was that way," Janine said. "And next year it will be that way again."

"I won't be president of anything at college," Todd observed wistfully.

"And nobody will know that I was the exchange student. They will probably be a dime a dozen at Berkeley—if I get in."

"Well, anyway, Janine," Todd told her. "Maybe Craig is in a different environment, where he doesn't seem so important. But he has still got to be just as important to you." Todd wanted to be sure Janine didn't fall out of love with Craig and decide to go for him. "Gosh, Craig is really crazy about you. And he's still the same great guy he was over at school. He really hasn't changed, himself. Just his surroundings and his status have changed. When he gets to be a senior, he will be a star again. So don't give up on him. Hey, Janine, you have the greatest guy in the world. Craig is a real prince."

"Oh, I wasn't giving up on him. I know how wonderful he is," Janine exclaimed. "I don't care whether he's a star. I always used to wish he wasn't, anyway, because that made him so hard to get. I just am afraid he isn't as happy over there and might feel lost in the crowd."

"Not him," Todd said. "He is not a guy who would ever be down. But I guess he misses you a lot and wishes you were over there. Hey, Janine, remember the letter I wrote you in Uruguay?"

"It was a nice letter, Todd. It made me feel good and bad. Good because it feels wonderful to know somebody likes you a lot, and bad because, you know, I had really fallen for Craig a long time before, and I couldn't return the affection you deserved. You have been such a good friend. That made me feel guilty, and so I didn't want to write you a disappointing answer." Todd looked over and saw a concerned frown on Janine's face.

"You don't need to worry about letting me down," Todd smiled. "Because right after I wrote you that letter, I met this girl, and I'm pretty much overboard for her, anyway. She and I are going to the beach tomorrow."

"Oh, Todd!" Janine looked genuinely pleased and surprised. "That's terrific. Who is she? I heard you and Jennifer Baines had been going around some."

"You heard wrong. Jennifer is okay, but she's not my type. I have only been to some parties where she is, but I don't go around with her at all. There's this other girl, who is really fantastic. I guess you might say I'm in love with her."

"Well, don't keep me in suspense, Todd. Who is she?"

"Her name is Heidi. She doesn't go to our school. She goes to Orchard High."

"Orchard High! How did you meet anyone from there?"

"It's kind of unbelievable. But there were these peacocks . . ." Todd went on to tell Janine how he had met Heidi.

"You know, I told you Craig was a prince. Well, Heidi is a princess. In fact, that's what a lot of people call her."

"Oh, Todd. I am dying to meet her."

"You might, someday. Only I'm still getting acquainted with her. We haven't known each other that long. Nobody knows about her except you; so don't mention her to anybody, not even Steve or Art or Sarah. I just wanted you to know so you wouldn't have to worry about my pestering you to be my girl."

Janine laughed, sounding relieved. "Todd, I might miss your pestering. It gives a girl's ego a boost to have an attractive guy interested. But, anyway, I always think of you as one of my best friends. I hope that won't change. We have had a lot of fun together."

They had turned off the highway now and were approaching Janine's house. Todd stopped the car. "Friends forever." He grinned at her, squeezing her hand. He took her up to her door, and before she went in, she stood on tiptoes and kissed his cheek.

"Thanks for everything," she said. "And your secret love is safe with me."

7

Todd's alarm woke him on Saturday before he was ready. He groaned, got out of bed, and splashed water on his face. Then, remembering what was in store—his date with Heidi—he was seized by a feeling of euphoria. A glance out the window told him the weather could have been better, but who would notice the weather when Heidi was around? He pulled on an Irish knit sweater over his jeans and grabbed a dark blue jacket with a hood from a peg in the closet. If you didn't have a hood, sometimes the sea breeze would freeze your ears off in this kind of weather. Todd stopped downstairs and made himself a tuna sandwich. He added an apple, an orange, and a couple of cans of soda and was on his way.

As he drove, he thought of what a good evening last night had turned out to be. All his problems with Janine had been smoothed out, and he and Janine were really great friends like they had always been. And he was getting in pretty solid with Craig Matthews, who, even if he wasn't a big shot at Berkeley, was still considered awesome at Blossom Valley High.

Todd was whistling and feeling really high when he drove up the Holmstroms' road. He almost ran over Zeus, the white peacock, who darted out between some shrubs onto the driveway. Todd had to put on the brakes fast, making a loud noise, and Zeus gave a loud squawk. Heidi heard them and ran out the front door. She was wearing white cords and a bright-blue hooded jacket.

"That was a close call," she shouted, her smile bringing out her dimples. Zeus had fanned out his tail and strutted angrily toward Todd's car as if to attack it.

"Wow, that's what I call spectacular!" Todd exclaimed, staring in awe at the delicately elegant white peacock.

"Come over here, Todd. If you look at him from this angle, you'll see the eyes in his tail."

"That peacock is pure white!" Todd objected. "What eyes?"

Heidi took his arm and pulled him to the right angle, and he could see the exquisite tracery of the white-on-white eye designs of the gorgeous peacock.

"You're right. He does have eyes on his tail. He looks pretty mad to me, though." Todd laughed.

"Peacocks will sometimes attack cars. They see their image in the hub caps, and that sets them off," Heidi said. "Come on in; we'll get my lunch, and you can say hi to Mom and Dad." Heidi moved like a whirlwind, darting into the kitchen to get her lunch, yelling into the back of the house.

"Mom, Dad. Todd's here. I'm about to leave."

Jackie wandered out, pulling a wagon with a kitten in it, and Jamie walked behind, pushing the kitten back in as it tried to escape from the wagon.

Mrs. Holmstrom came in from the backyard with a

fragrant bouquet of china-lilies, and then Dr. Holmstrom appeared from one of the rooms.

"Where are you youngsters going?" he asked.

"Down to Pescadero or one of those beaches along there."

"Not the greatest beach weather," he commented.

"I missed the shorebird field trip," Todd told Dr. Holmstrom. "I had to take this test to get in college. So Heidi is going to show me the shorebirds today."

"Should be a lot out today. Godwits, killdeers—watch for turnstones and oyster catchers. You might even spot some murres down there. Don't forget your binoculars."

"Oh, I was about to. I'm so excited." Heidi looked up at Todd with a quick smile and whirled off to get the binoculars. Then they were on their way. Alone at last! Todd looked at his companion. She had her hood up so that her hair wasn't showing, only her face. She smiled. "It's really happening. I was afraid something would interfere again," she said.

"No way. Never again." They wound through the woods.

"You won't have any trouble about keeping the car all day?"

"No, 'cause my mom and dad have gone to a weekend convention. My aunt is staying with us, and she has her own car."

"We can stay as long as we like then."

"Just so I get home by 5:30. I have to get over to the pizzeria."

"That gives us all day."

They chose one of a long line of connected beaches. "We can run and hike for miles along here," Heidi said. Here and there along the smooth, surf-edged sand, rocky promontories jutted into the sea. "Those rocky places might have some oyster catchers or turnstones in them," Heidi commented. Behind the sandy beaches, huge rock cliffs rose. Todd's car was parked on one of them, and he and Heidi descended, their lunches and other gear in back-packs.

"The beaches are practically deserted today," Todd said.

"Some people are scared off by the weather," Heidi said. "But I like it. I like to see big waves and to walk by the sea in the rain."

A flock of birds, all moving in unison, chased the surf down to the sea. They looked like so many wind-up toys as the surf chased them back up the beach.

"Those sandpipers look like they're on wheels," Todd laughed. Todd and Heidi watched the sandpi-pers moving in rhythm with the surf, quickly pecking at some invisible food in the ocean's wake.

"Hey, Heidi. Look. Out there on that breaker. What kind of bird is that?"

Heidi put up her binoculars. "That's not a bird, it's a foot."

"You're right." Todd also looked through the field glasses. "There's another foot." Todd watched as the feet were joined by a supine, brown furry body and a large triangular head. The creature rocked between two waves.

"A sea otter!" Heidi exulted. "And so close to shore!"

Todd and Heidi viewed the otter rocking in the cradle of a wave for a time and held their breaths when a big comber rolled up behind the otter's tranquil hammock, flinging the furry creature face-down into the sand.

"Ooops! Hey, he doesn't look like that even fazed him!" Todd saw the otter twist back into the waves and reappear, floating on his back, holding in his paw a treasure he had garnered from the surf.

"He must have caught a clam!" Heidi exclaimed.

Her hand reached out and touched Todd's, and he enclosed it in his. The otter was beating the clam on his stomach with gusto as he lay back on his water-bed.

"Can you see, Todd," Heidi said, peering through the binoculars, "that he has a rock on his stomach to break the clam shell?" The otter ate the clam and rocked some more on the undulations of the sea.

Todd held Heidi's hand tightly. It was so smooth and soft, he never wanted to let it go. The otter again writhed beneath the sea and came up with a second course, making a pounding board of his stomach. Then he seemed to drift backward through the waves, and Heidi and Todd walked on down the beach, not saying anything, still holding hands.

Todd pointed out a group of mottled brown birds with long legs and very long beaks. They were busily probing their beaks into the sand. "What are those characters?" he asked Heidi.

"Marbled godwits," Heidi told him. "I'll tell you how to identify it. You see, when it pulls its beak out of the sand, it has a slight upcurve to it."

"What are they digging for?"

"There are all kinds of organisms under the sand. Crabs and other crustaceans, insects, worms. And nature has arranged it so that all the shorebirds will get their share. Those tiny sandpipers have little short beaks. They get what's in the top of the sand. The godwits get something much farther down that's not on the sandpiper's diet." Heidi let out a peal of laughter. "You know what? I sound just like my dad! I've heard him lecture so often on shorebirds that I think I've memorized his spiel."

"You really know a lot," Todd said admiringly. "That godwit over there has got to have the prize beak," Todd laughed. "He looks like Pinocchio." He pointed out a large, long-legged brown speckled bird whose beak was almost as long as his body.

"That's not a godwit," Heidi objected. "That is a long-billed curlew. Didn't I just tell you the godwit's beak curves up? And this one curves down. So he's a curlew."

"I'm getting overwhelmed," Todd said. "There're too many different kinds of birds that all look pretty much alike."

"Then let's run." Heidi wrested her hand from Todd's and started off down the beach. Todd took out after her and soon they were running at top speed. Heidi was fast. It took all Todd's energy to outpace her. After a while Todd collapsed breathlessly on a rocky outcropping that led into the sea. Heidi was panting hard when she joined him.

"Hey, no fair," she said. "You have longer legs than I have."

"You can really run," Todd panted.

"I'm going to beat you on the next lap," Heidi promised.

Among the rocks, Heidi spied a black turnstone to show Todd. "Some of the shorebirds stay in the rocks instead of on the beaches," she explained. "They find their food in the crevices and under rocks. You can see that the turnstone has a short, strong beak with a little upturned point. He uses it to turn over stones and find insects or crabs under them." The slate-colored bird scurried away without Todd's seeing it turn over a rock.

Wandering on down the beach, they saw surfbirds, dowitchers, yellowlegs, willets, and a great variety of sandpipers. "Actually, the godwits and the curlews and a lot of these other birds are all in the sandpiper family," she told him. They passed a group of birds with white underparts and two heavy black bands around their necks. "Killdeers," Heidi said. She ran toward the group, and they took flight, uttering the sound "Killdeer."

"These birds are famous for pretending they have

111

a broken wing when they are trying to protect their young," she added. "But the killdeer isn't one of the sandpiper family. It's a plover."

"Heidi, you better not ask me what anything is on the way back, 'cause I'm saturated with shorebirds up to here. I won't know one from the other. They're getting all jumbled up in my head."

"Okay. Lesson's over," Heidi agreed. "You want to build a sand castle?"

"Sure," Todd assented. They chose a place where the sand looked wet and sticky, and they began digging and piling up sand, constructing turrets, moats, and making bridges with pieces of driftwood. Heidi collected feathers and put plumes on top of the turrets. They built roads leading into the castle. Todd felt all of his responsibilities—his presidential duties, his job at the pizzeria, his efforts to get good grades this year—had been lifted off him, and he could just enjoy.

"You're the sleeping beauty in the castle," Todd told Heidi.

"And you're the prince."

"Do I get to wake you with a kiss?" Todd moved over to where Heidi was crouched in the sand smoothing out a road. Her tempting lips curved in a smile.

"Not unless you catch me." She sprang up and sprinted down to the surf. She kicked off her shoes and rolled up the legs of her cords and started wading into the foam.

"Hey, Heidi. It's too cold. It's winter, remember?" Todd objected, moving Heidi's shoes and socks further up the beach. "The surf is going to get your shoes if you're not more careful."

Heidi had waded into the sea up to her knees, and as she ran back, a big wave crashed to shore. The sky was a gunmetal gray, and the sea looked leaden and ominous.

112

Heidi ran in again. "Sure, it's cold," she conceded. "But it's bearable. Come on, Todd."

"Heidi," Todd said, as his common sense posted a warning, "those waves are a lot higher than usual. You've gotta be careful. Come on out, 'cause I'm not coming in." Todd did not like the implication that he was chicken, but he refused to let Heidi taunt him into foolhardiness. The daring, impulsive side of her nature was something he had not seen. She was teasing him. He fought against taking off his own shoes, going in, seizing her, and kissing some caution into her.

And then Heidi, running ahead of a thundering wave that crashed about her, let out a strange cry, leaned and bundled up something in her arms and ran toward Todd, bent under the weight of her burden. Todd hurried to meet her. He saw a long, webbed foot dangling from her untidy burden.

"What on earth? Is it alive?"

"Probably not."

Todd took the feathery bundle from Heidi and put it on the sand. "It's some big bird that got tangled up in a fishing line."

"Look at that beak! It's a pelican!" Heidi said. "Quick, let's untangle it."

"It's alive," Todd said. "Its eye opened." Todd saw that the bird had upper and lower eyelids that opened like a camera shutter, both from the top and bottom, to reveal a sharp, yellow-ringed eye.

They found the end of the fishing line. The pelican had obviously snapped it off and wound itself up in it in struggling to get free.

"The fishhook is stuck in the pouch under its beak," Todd said.

"Don't hurt him," Heidi cautioned.

"I know how to get out fishhooks. I've been fishing with my dad a lot," Todd said. He delicately pressed a prong on the hook, and it popped out of the leathery skin of the pelican's pouch. Above the pelican's eyes, there was a crest of yellowish feathers, coming to a little point in back. Heidi stroked the bird's head as Todd tried to untangle the nylon wire. Her fingers moved gently down the white feathers of the pelican's long neck.

"Do you think he's okay?" she asked anxiously.

"Well, he's not dead. But he might have broken something struggling with that line." The wire bound the pelican's long, powerful beak down against its chest, and its wings and one leg were also bound against its body. As Todd untangled the line, the bird's beak was freed, and it lifted its head, opened its beak, and fanned out its pouch. Its upper beak had a little hook on the end.

The frightened pelican snapped at Todd, its eyes flashing in the circle of bare skin around them.

"Wow! He could do some damage with that beak!" Todd exclaimed. One of the bird's legs was freed then, and that appendage, which was short and sturdy above the huge brown webbed foot, kicked out vigorously. "Well, anyway, that leg isn't broken," Todd said.

As he unwound, Heidi held the huge bird, which must have weighed twenty pounds.

"We'll have to keep a good grip on him as he gets free," Heidi said. "He'll probably struggle." She continued to stroke the bird, and its eye opened and closed drowsily. "I think this pelican is beginning to trust us, though," she added.

Now Todd had a wing free. The pelican unfolded its long brown wing and stretched it to its full length.

"Awesome," Todd said. "That wing must be four feet long."

"And it's okay," Heidi crowed. "Nothing seems to be broken, none of its flight feathers."

"That's about it," Todd said, pulling the last

strand of fishing wire from the other wing of the bird, as Heidi held the wing down. The bird did not struggle, but stayed docilely in their hands.

"It likes us," Heidi said. "I never imagined when we came out here that I would get to pet a pelican."

"Who could ever dream of seeing one so close up—the details of how its pouch is made, and all?" Todd said, touching the horizontally-ribbed, tough elastic skin that hung below the pelican's lower beak, feeling the texture of it, smelling the briny aroma of the giant seabird.

Now the pelican's head began to dart nervously back and forth. "He's ready to go," Heidi said. "We better set him free."

"Bon voyage, pelican. Watch out for those fishing lines," Todd admonished.

"Let's carry him over to the surf where I found him," Heidi suggested, and they trudged with the big bird down to the edge of foam. The pelican stood awkwardly on his tremendous feet and extended his wings to full span as Heidi and Todd stood back. The sea swirled about his feet, and he ran clumsily, his huge wings flapping through the mist and surf.

When at last he was airborne, Todd looked over and saw tears glistening in Heidi's eyes. He put his arm around her and pulled her close to him. They watched the bird soaring. Nothing had ever exhilarated Todd so much. He felt joy surging through him.

"Free to live!" Heidi exulted. "It's fate that we happened to pass this place just as the pelican was tossed to shore."

"Somebody upstairs was watching," Todd agreed. "Those terrific wings could have been grounded forever."

Todd and Heidi walked slowly down the beach encircled in each other's arms, awed at the rare moment shared with a wild creature and the sudden consciousness of the precious and ephemeral nature of life.

They were walking close to the surf, and they saw a big flock of tiny sandpipers run suddenly up the beach. There was a whoosh of surf, and a cold wave took them by surprise, drenching them to the knees.

"Darn," Todd complained, "now our shoes are all soaked." As they moved farther up the beach, Todd saw that there was a strange, greenish cast to the sky. "I'm afraid we're in for heavy weather," he said uneasily. "Maybe we better not stay out too long."

"As for me, I'm hungry," Heidi said. She shivered, for the wind had turned cold and her clothes were wet.

"Me, too. Let's go up against the cliffs and eat," Todd agreed. The huge cliffs stretched in an unbroken line along the beach, perforated here and there by caves halfway up their height.

"I know what would be fun. Let's eat in one of the caves."

"Did you bring a ladder?" Todd asked. "How would we get up there?"

"Those cliffs aren't hard to climb. Have you ever done any mountaineering?" Heidi asked.

"Not really. I climbed around in the Sierras some, but no place that really takes skill."

"Dad taught me a lot about climbing," Heidi said with confidence, standing below the cliff and looking up at a yawning cave. "We would be protected from the wind up there. It would be a neat place to eat lunch."

"It looks pretty inaccessible to me." Todd shook his head, amazed again at Heidi's daring. She was examining the cliff minutely.

"Piece of cake," she announced. Todd watched in astonishment as Heidi's feet and hands found heretofore invisible knobs and depressions in the cliff, gaining a foothold and clinging to impossible folds in the rock.

Before Todd's incredulous eyes, Heidi's hand reached the opening of the cave, and soon she stood triumphantly in it.

"It's bigger than you would think," she yelled down exultantly. "We can go over behind the wall here and eat. There's a kind of rock bench. Come on."

"Hey, Heidi," Todd looked perplexed. "Maybe you're the human fly, but I never took any mountaineering lessons."

"You're about to," Heidi laughed. "Just find a place where your toe will fit in. There are plenty of places big enough to get a toehold. Then find another place that's big enough for your hand to get a grip."

"I'm heavier than you."

"Try, anyway. It's fun up here. So what if you fall? You'll just hit the sand, and it's soft. You can't fall far."

"Oh, well, okay," Todd grumbled. "Here goes a cliffhanger."

Todd saw Heidi's face laughing down at him like a magnet pulling him up the cliff. He found a place where his toe fit precariously and then grabbed onto a questionable-looking knob of rock. He might break it off. Another toehold and handhold, and he was spread-eagled against the rock. "Now what?" he asked. "I can't even see."

"Now move up one foot and then one hand, and you'll gradually be here. I'll reach down a hand when you're getting close."

Todd gained a few feet, his hands raw against the rough rock. Then he fell back to the sand and had to start over.

"Come on! You were doing great!" Heidi encouraged. Todd looked up again from the place where he was sprawled on the sand. Heidi's laughing face, beckoning but still mocking him a little, aroused a combination of anger and determination in him. Why had she done such an impossible thing? They could just as well have eaten lunch down here on the sand. But he was not going to let her show him up. If she could do it, he could.

The tenderness of Todd's hands, aggravated by the wind, which was becoming bitingly cold, intensified the urgency he felt to make it into the cave, and this time he went slowly, trying to control his breathing so his body wouldn't jerk away from the cliff.

"You're almost here. One more step up, and this time, you're going to grab the cave mouth. I'll guide your hand," Heidi said excitedly.

Todd took a deep breath and proceeded with caution. He felt Heidi's smooth hand on his, and then his fingers curled around the cave entrance under her guidance. He braced his left foot, and now both hands were up.

"You made it!" Heidi's exultation was contagious and sent a surge of strength through Todd that carried his body up over the cave entrance, and he slid in on his stomach.

"Whew!" He looked up into Heidi's deep blue eyes.

"See," she said, "if we had eaten on the beach, we would have been freezing in that wind." They could hear the wind now, making a hollow whoosh as it passed the cave mouth. "And it would have blown sand in our food." Heidi was shrugging the straps off her backpack. Todd sat up and did the same, slumping against the rock of the cave wall, giving an exaggerated show of exhaustion.

"Isn't this fun?" Heidi's eyes sparkled, and her dimples flashed. "Let's pretend it's a zillion years ago and we're cavemen. Nothing exists in the modern world."

"And these aren't tuna fish sandwiches," Todd added, "but an actual hunk of raw tuna that we just clubbed out of the sea."

"Ugh!" Heidi grimaced. "Mine came from a bolognasaurus."

They both laughed.

"Maybe this is a seal's home, and we'll be evicted," Todd speculated.

"Stupid. A seal could never get up here with its flippers!" Heidi's bubbly mirth echoed through the cave.

Heidi munched on her bologna sandwich and Todd on his tuna. "The sea air makes me ravenous. I wish I had brought more food," he said.

"I have a whole package of brownies. Help yourself." Heidi extended the package.

"Wow, I could really pig out on these," Todd said. Heidi was taking off her jacket because it was damp and she wanted to dry it out. Her silvery-blonde hair flowed around her shoulders, framing her animated dark eyes as she chattered. Todd planned his strategy to kiss her. He had to do it before leaving the cave, because it was an ideal place. Isolated, cozy, shadowy. This date was coming out pretty well, in spite of the weather, and Todd thought he saw signs that Heidi would welcome a kiss. He was deciding whether he should move to the right side or the left side of Heidi, since he was now sitting opposite her. He decided he would move on the outside, toward the cave mouth, and then seize her in his arms and . . .

Heidi had spread her jacket out on some rocks to dry. Her blouse was a little wet, too, so that it was plastered against her. Todd tried hard not to look too much, or to think of what it might feel like to touch her. He had to be careful. After all, she was a professor's daughter. He was just going to kiss her very gently at first, and then maybe he could tell if she wanted him to try anything else. He had a feeling she would be pretty disappointed if they were in a cave alone and nothing at all happened.

Todd began his move. He started to slither around the cave mouth so he would be sitting beside her. As he passed the cave entrance, he was suddenly conscious that the sea did not have its accustomed rhythm—the crashing of the breaker, the hollow roar as the surf receded, and then an intervening silence. There was no rhythm at all, but just an uninterrupted pounding and sloshing. It was eerie. Instead of moving on in pursuit of Heidi, Todd leaned out over the mouth of the cave, and his skin prickled with instant fear at what he saw. The beach over which they had just frolicked had disappeared. The sea had covered it, and it lay about six feet below the cave, swirling angrily. Out beyond, huge swells rose into mountainous iron-gray breakers that raced in to crash against the cliffs. He and Heidi were trapped! There was no way they could get out of the cave!

8

Heidi still lounged in her comfortable crevice against the cave wall. "Is that rain coming in?" she asked lazily. "If it is, I guess we better start back. Or do you think we should just wait here till it stops?"

Todd looked quickly toward Heidi and then away. She was so innocent and beautiful. He didn't want to tell her. He took a deep breath, trying to dissolve the hard knot of terror that gripped his abdomen.

"It's only 2:30," Heidi went on. "I guess we have plenty of time to wait, but we don't need to. I'm getting kind of tired of the cave, and besides, I like to walk on the beach in the rain. But it might be later than 2:30. I might have gotten my watch wet when we picked up the pelican. It might have stopped." She held her watch up to her ear.

Todd's eyes were round and glazed with fear. A rush of adrenalin stiffened his body as he looked at Heidi.

"What's the matter, Todd? You look like you've seen a sea monster!"

"I wish that was it. But, Heidi, the tide has come up. There isn't any beach to walk on."

"You're putting me on, Todd Roberts."

Tears of desperation moistened Todd's eyes. "I wish I were."

Alarmed now, Heidi pushed past him to look below. The angry wind whipped her long hair wildly back into the cave, and she closed her eyes against the salty rain that bit into her skin.

"Wow, that's incredible! What do we do now?"

"The only way we could get out would be to fly."

"The tide isn't supposed to come up this high. But, anyway, it will go back down again, and then we can get out. In six hours, it will be low tide again. So probably in about four hours, we will have some kind of a strip of beach to walk on."

"There's a big storm involved, too, Heidi. It may not work out in the regular way. The waves are like the Rocky Mountains out there."

"The storm will die down, too. They don't last forever."

Todd was silent, and he felt a wince of pain as he looked at Heidi's perfect, untroubled face. She refused to be perturbed.

"So we have to stay up here a few more hours. So what? We're just lucky we're up here and not down there."

Todd looked down again. The sea boiled about eight feet below them. Out in the misty gray distance, it swelled ominously. Down the long line of cliffs, he could see towering columns of water fragmented into spray as the sea flung itself angrily against the granite.

Heidi was searching in her backpack. "A couple of weeks ago, I went over to spend the night with my girlfriend, and I took a deck of cards in my backpack. I hope I didn't leave them at her house. We could play some gin rummy if they're in here. That might help to take your mind off the storm, Todd. If you could see your face! Your eyes are practically bugging out of your head with fright."

Todd wished he were the cool one, that he could be trying to calm Heidi down, that she couldn't see his face. She might not think it was manly to be so scared. "Gosh, Heidi, I feel responsible. I brought you out here, and I'm responsible for getting you back."

"You will. Just relax and the storm will die down. Besides, why should you be the one responsible? I came out here on my own. In fact, I was the one who suggested going up in the cave, wasn't I? If we hadn't come up here we would have seen the tide rising, and we would have had time to get back to the car."

"The car is really far away," Todd remembered. "We hiked a long way. More than an hour, didn't we? Past all those godwits and turnstones. Remember when we made the sand castle? It's completely wiped out now."

"Yeah. And then there was the pelican. At least he's not trapped anymore. He can just fly away from the storm."

"Where do pelicans go, anyway, in a storm? Do they roost somewhere, or just sit around in the waves? Or fly someplace where there's no storm?"

"I don't know. I'd have to ask Dad."

Todd thought about Heidi's dad and hoped they wouldn't have to stay in the cave long enough to worry him.

"I *do* have my deck of cards. We can play gin!" Heidi took out some worn playing cards secured by a rubber band. "I also have my field guide to birds in here. I'll show you pictures of the ones we saw, and that will fix them in your mind."

Todd felt himself calming down. His love for her swept over him as the sea was sweeping up the cliffs. He was flooded with love, and it temporarily chased away his fear.

"It's pretty wet here in the entrance where the rain has been coming in." Todd could taste salt spray on his lips, and he remembered his plot to kiss Heidi. It didn't seem quite as appropriate now.

"Up here on the ledge, it's dry," Heidi said, shuffling the cards. They played for a while, forgetting their plight as they competed in the card game.

"Hey, you're quite a card sharp," Todd complained when Heidi had won several games in succession. She flashed her heart-wrenching smile at him. He didn't really want to play gin rummy anymore, but he wanted to keep Heidi amused so she wouldn't be able to think about the implications of their situation. Todd stealthily cast a look below him between games, and his heart leaped into his throat as he saw that the ocean had risen a couple of feet above its previous level. Now and then an angry wave would slosh through the cave entrance, and there was a puddle of water below the ledge on which Heidi and Todd were sitting.

"Let me show you some card tricks. Maybe you didn't know that I'm both a magician and a juggler." He took up three stones from the cave floor and displayed his juggling technique. Then he asked Heidi to pick a card and mystified her with his ability to guess it, picking it out of the hood of her jacket and doing other diverting tricks. He told her a few of his best jokes, but then he began to run out of amusements and started to brood again about the advancing ocean and the continual roar of the wind and crashing of the waves outside the cave.

"My watch really did stop." Heidi showed Todd that the hands still pointed to two-thirty. "It's probably much later than we suspected. In fact, it's beginning to get dark."

"It's just the storm. It couldn't really be that late. The clouds are just so heavy," Todd consoled without conviction.

"No, it's really getting to be night. If we don't get out soon, it is going to be dark." Heidi's confident voice was showing a touch of panic.

"Storms don't last forever. You said so yourself," he reminded her. "It will have to stop pretty soon."

"You know what?" Heidi had a sudden inspiration. "We could get out the same way we got in. Climb up the rest of the cliff. Only we have to do it while there's still some light and we can see the footholds."

"No way!" Todd said, scowling sternly at Heidi. "That would be guaranteed suicide."

"We got up here that way," Heidi said defiantly. "And it's just about as far up to the top of the cliff as it was from the beach to the cave. I'm going to try it."

"Heidi, you had the sand to fall into before. What if you slipped trying to make it to the top? Look what you'd fall into." The sea swirled angrily beneath them. "You could get zapped by a wave. If those waves can cut caves into the granite, think of what they could do to you."

"You're such a pessimist—so negative," Heidi said. "It's our only way of escape. Don't you see that the sea is still rising? Why should we sit here and get drowned when we have a chance to get out?"

"Fat chance!" Todd said. "Forget that, Heidi."

"Maybe you are too chicken to try it, but I'm not."

"I think you're getting stir-crazy, Heidi," Todd countered. He was worried at the tremulous tone of her voice. Her usual sunny disposition and level-headed approach to problems seemed to have been swept out by the storm.

"Anyway, here goes!" Heidi stood in the cave mouth, and with one foot inside the cave, she swung the other out, clinging to the entrance, trying to gain a foothold.

Todd made a lunge for her, grabbing her around the waist to pull her in. He could feel her shivering. She struggled against him, almost pulling him out of the cave into the sea. Todd got a sick feeling as he thought of their hurtling together into the roiling, seething sea, which lay like a witch's cauldron beneath the cave. Mustering all his strength, he yanked Heidi's arms away from the entrance. As he held her struggling figure against him, trying to force her back into the cave, a giant wave slapped against the entrance, bringing on instant darkness, and all the fight went out of Heidi's body. Todd felt her become limp in his arms. Then there was a terrifying withdrawal of the air from the cave as the wave was sucked back from the sea. The cave became a vacuum, and Todd dragged Heidi back behind the cave mouth. He felt electrified by the disappearance of air from the cave. He could almost feel his hair standing on end.

"There, you see. If you had gone out, the wave would have sucked you off the cliff."

Todd lifted Heidi up on the ledge. The wave had left a pool of water on the cave floor. Then he hoisted himself up on the ledge beside her.

"That was a crazy thing to do. I just suddenly felt desperate," Heidi told him.

"We're both soaking wet now," Todd complained. "If we had stayed back here, at least we would've been dry."

"I keep making things worse and worse," Heidi admitted.

Todd held her in his arms, and she pressed her

face against his shoulder and started to cry. Todd remembered reading a newspaper story once about some people who had been trapped in a cave in the sea cliffs. Had they died? Had they been rescued? He couldn't remember which. The sea was lapping up the ledge. There was a chance that he and Heidi could die. It was the first time Todd had ever considered dying. He held Heidi a little closer, and thought about how bad it would be for Aunt Margaret, who was supposed to be looking after him and Sandy. He thought about Ken Garcia taking over as president of the senior class. He wondered what was going on at the pizzeria. Darkness was falling. It was time for him to be there. The owner was probably cursing him out for not showing up. Little did he know that Todd's life might be snuffed out by the sea any minute now. He thought of all the people who would be affected. Janine and Craig would be shocked. Only last night, we were all having fun, they would think, and now he's gone. The biology report on his desk, which he had to turn in on Monday, wouldn't get finished. His mom and dad were living it up at their convention, little suspecting the fate that was overtaking their son.

As the last ray of light disappeared from the cave, Todd's melancholy deepened. As long as he had so little life to live now—maybe only an hour or two—he might as well enjoy what was left. He put his hand gently under Heidi's chin and turned her face up to press his mouth to hers, very tenderly so he wouldn't upset her further. Her lips were smooth, but cold and salty. Then he could feel her answering pressure, as if she had been waiting for his kiss. She snuggled closer to him. He could feel from the sound of her voice that her tears had been replaced by her dimply smile. "Oh, Todd," she said. "I didn't mean to be so gloomy. I just got scared for a minute, but it's okay now. Being so close to you makes it better."

"Yeah, I know. It is scary, but it will be all right after a while." Todd was overcome with love for her, and he kissed her again. This time her lips were warm and responsive. Kissing Heidi made him forget about dying, so he kept doing it, with longer and deeper kisses.

"I guess you can tell I'm pretty crazy about you, Heidi," he said huskily.

"I've gotten that way about you, too," she answered.

Todd held her close in the clammy darkness, wishing he could produce a magic carpet and fly them out of danger. The sea still thundered and crashed outside the cave. The cave smelled strongly of fish and seaweed.

Heidi recovered some of her animation. "I just thought," she exclaimed. "That night I took my backpack over to my girlfriend's, I had a flashlight in there 'cause I walked over in the dark. I bet I still have it." She groped for the backpack and found the flashlight. She turned it on Todd and laughed. "I just wanted to see if you were still real."

Todd could see the contours of her face and her big, velvety eyes in the dimness. The circle of light played into the cave mouth, where they could see the remnants of foam and spray from a wave that had just crashed. The ocean was up to their ledge. Heidi set the flashlight on its end so that its beam hit the rough ceiling of the cave.

"I have something in my pack, too," Todd remembered. "An extra soda from lunch."

"Maybe we didn't eat all those brownies," Heidi hoped. "Then we could have dinner."

There were three brownies left of the original dozen, and Todd and Heidi shared the soda and each ate a brownie. They put the other one away for any later emergency. Todd had a fleeting thought that this might be his last meal.

Heidi got out her bird guide, and turning the flashlight on it, she read Todd some of the descriptions of the birds they had seen.

"Do you remember the dowitcher?" Heidi asked.

"Is it the one with the beak that curves up or down?"

"Neither. It has a straight beak. And it doesn't have a long neck like the godwits and curlews. It has shorter legs, too."

"You know, Heidi, all these shorebirds—now that there's no shore, where are they? They can't chase the ocean back and forth up the beach when there's no beach."

"Maybe they're waiting out the storm in the next cave." Heidi laughed. Todd was glad to hear her laugh. Then she wasn't scared anymore—or, like him, she had just simply accepted the situation as something they couldn't do anything about and had relaxed.

After a while, however, Todd felt himself tensing up again, for over on his side of the rough stone bench, the water was rising. The whole cave floor had a foot of water in it now, and frequently waves would slosh in. He tried to ignore it and not to alarm Heidi when he said, "Let's move over to the other end of the ledge," for the ledge slanted upward a few inches, and Todd was practically sitting in water.

Heidi's eyes looked enormous in the dim light of the torch, and as they settled into the upper corner of the cave, Todd kissed Heidi again and then again. "It's going to be okay," he said, holding her close. She put her arms around his neck. "If anything bad happens, I'm glad I was with you when it did," she said.

Todd experienced mixed feelings of joy that Heidi returned his affection and fear that a huge wave might sweep them out of the cave into eternity at any moment.

They were silent for a while, and then Todd said, "I know this might not be the time or place to bring the subject up, but I was just curious."

"What about?"

"There was that guy Joe I saw you with at the pizzeria. I got a kind of impression that he might be a pretty steady boyfriend of yours, and I was just wondering . . ."

"Joe?" Heidi sounded astonished and a little outraged that the name should have come up in the sanctity of what might be their last moments on earth.

"Yeah. I just wondered where he stood. You know, on account of me being so crazy about you, it just worried me a little."

"You can quit worrying. Joe is a guy I have known since the year one. Would you believe he just about latched onto me in kindergarten? He has been hanging around ever since. You saw him. He is a pretty big and aggressive guy. All through grade school and high school, he has made a point of intimidating anybody else that got near me, and so I have hardly been able to even get to know any other guys. At the school parties, it was always assumed I would go with him. Nobody else would even think of asking me. I've gotten pretty bored with his monopolizing, and lots of times I just would rather not go anywhere than go out with him, and I just tell him I have to do something with my family."

"Then he is the only guy you go out with?"

"I couldn't believe my good luck when I met you. A cute guy who goes to another school. Somebody Joe couldn't psych out of my life."

"You like me better than him, then?"

"Can't you tell by now?" Heidi cuddled close to him, and they kissed again.

"I was going to the movies with him and the gang

130

tonight. Just about the same kids you saw me with at the pizza parlor. We have a good time and all, and he isn't mean or anything—just boring. I wonder what Mom and Dad will say when I don't get home. They'll probably have the police out looking for us."

"A lot of good it will do, unless they had some police with fins. My Aunt Margaret is probably going loco. She might have even called my folks in Denver. What a mess!"

"Really." Heidi sounded drowsy. "Oh, Todd, I'm so cold and sleepy."

Todd laughed uneasily. "I wish I could put a log on the fire. But do you think you could just lean on me and get a little sleep? I'll be here guarding you from invading sharks."

"It's hard to sleep when it's so cold. We should have brought some blankets."

"A lot of good that would do. They would be soaking wet by now, like we are."

Heidi leaned against Todd's shoulder and shut her eyes. Looking down at her, Todd thought futilely of how he could save her. He thought of blasting off the top of the cave to make a big escape hatch and of carrying Heidi through it. He imagined a big redwood log floating through the entrance on which he and Heidi would ride to safety. He dozed off himself and dreamed of a big pelican swimming in to carry them off on its back. He came awake with a start at the noise of a huge wave that slapped against the cave mouth and left another foot of icy water sloshing about their legs. Todd tried to keep the flashlight and their backpacks over the ledge. The water was almost to their waists. A few more waves like that and . . . Todd leaned down and kissed the top of Heidi's head. He was glad she was asleep. It was scary to be conscious.

Outside, the gale still whistled and howled relentlessly. People were missing them now, Todd knew, but what could they do? They couldn't send the Coast Guard out for them, because no boat or ship could navigate in such a wild sea. A helicopter couldn't fly in such weather, either. Besides, nobody would know where to look. Todd's car was way down the beach. He pictured it sitting there, being lashed by the wind and rain. It was miles away. Even if he and Heidi ever got out of this cave alive, they wouldn't be able to make it down to the car after this ordeal.

Todd thought longingly of his room and his bed. He might never see them again. He imagined making himself hot chocolate. In the darkness, he felt something slithery and slimy beneath his elbow. He touched it fearfully. But it was only a piece of leathery seaweed, which had floated in. What other inhabitants of the sea might be in the cave with them? Eels? Octopi? The sea could have swept anything in.

Todd fought drowsiness. As helpless as he was, he could not risk falling asleep. She might slip off the ledge into the pool of water below and drown. Water was slowly filling the cave. They might soon have to stand to keep their heads above water. Heidi was shorter than he was. He might even have to hold her up to keep her from going under before he did—put her up on his shoulders, or something. He wondered if he had the strength.

Once the cave filled with water clear up to their shoulders, but then it receded from the cave. The sudden inundation brought Heidi awake. She couldn't figure out for a time where she was. Todd turned on the flashlight, and slowly Heidi remembered their plight. She shivered and her teeth chattered. Todd feared she was getting sick and he wasn't in very good shape himself.

His ears had become attuned to the sounds of the storm—the moaning and shrieking of the wind and the crash and thunder of the sea. Now he felt that the storm was diminishing. Either that, or his ears had been affected so that he couldn't hear much anymore.

"I think the storm is dying down, Heidi," he said, but she didn't answer; she just drooped dispiritedly against his shoulder. Todd turned off the flashlight. He didn't want to run down the battery. They sat in silence and dark for a while.

The ocean swelled now and then up to their shoulders. There were only a few feet left between them and the top of the cave.

"Do you think you can stand up, Heidi?" Todd asked gently. "You can lean against me." Heidi wearily got to her feet. She stood on the far end of the ledge, which slanted up. Todd stood beside her with his arms around her. It would be easy for them to slip, because of all that slimy seaweed and stuff the ocean was hurling into the cave.

They stood in silence, Todd supporting Heidi and wondering when his legs would give out and they would both disappear into the water, which ebbed and rose irregularly. Slowly the top of the cave became visible.

"It's getting to be morning," Todd said. Heidi didn't answer. Her eyes were closed, and a surge of fear animated Todd. Was she becoming unconscious? He shook her. Her eyelids opened a slit and then closed. She was practically a dead weight against him. The water was up to her shoulders, and he had to keep her standing up. He struggled to keep his will alive. It could be a matter of minutes before the sea filled their cave completely, and there was little strength left in his muscles. It would be so easy to let go and just let the relentless sea take over. He had to keep Heidi up, no matter how painful the effort.

Was it just his imagination, or was the wind diminishing? Todd thought that the nerve-racking ceaseless howling and shrieking were softening and modifying, that the sea was not being hurled against the cliff with such furious intensity. A little more light entered what was left of the cave, which almost made Todd wish they had been left in darkness, for it revealed the lead-gray water, sprinkled with ragged fragments of flotsam, and he could see how the storm had devastated Heidi. Her large, dark blue eyes were closed, and all the animation and freshness had left her face. Her hair had lost its light and vibrance and clung, dank and salty, about her. Todd shook her again.

She opened her eyes. "Have I been asleep?" she asked.

"Try to stay awake, Heidi, because we have to keep standing."

"There isn't really any use, is there?" she asked tonelessly.

"Of course there is!" He mustered up enough energy to give a fake show of optimism. "Pretty soon, we'll just swim out, and then the ocean will reach the top of the cliff; then we'll be back on dry land, get into the car, and drive back home." He thought he saw the start of a smile, which Heidi didn't have the strength or the will to finish. He loved her way down into the very nuclei of his cells.

"You know what?" he said a little later. "The ocean may be going down. It was clear up to our shoulders, and it's not anymore." The water line had dropped to the middle of his chest.

"Maybe low tide is on its way."

"I don't know whether it's the tide or the storm dying out." Todd looked out of what remained of the cave entrance, for the morning light now made the surface of the sea visible. The wind was definitely moderating and the ocean becoming more calm. A gull flapped past the cave entrance, and the gray light filtered through a light slanting rain.

"It doesn't really change our circumstances much," Heidi observed.

"Well, anyway, hang in there. The sea came up here pretty suddenly. It could go back the same way." Todd racked his brain to think of ways to amuse Heidi and keep up her spirits. Clowning was out—impossible when you're chest-deep in water. Should he tell her again how much he loved her? Even love seemed out of place when survival was the question. They didn't speak for a while, and then into the pelting of the rain, the crashing of waves, the sloshing and slapping of water against the cave walls, a new sound intruded: a sound of a rough-running motor. It grew louder and then diminished.

"Heidi, I think a helicopter just passed along the cliff," Todd said hesitantly.

"I heard. But how could they know we were in here?"

"They couldn't. Anyway, it's good news. I know they're looking for us. They must have spotted my car."

"Miles down the cliffs. And they probably think we're drowned, and they'll give up."

"No, Heidi. The good thing is that the weather is okay for a helicopter to fly in."

Heidi revived a little and seemed to gather some hope. "I know what. You have the bright red backpack, Todd. Is there any way we could hang it out of the cave so they can tell where we are?"

"Great idea!" Todd yelled. His voice formed a ripply echo in the cave. "I don't know how we'll hang it out, but that would sure put us on the map."

"*If* the helicopter comes back," Heidi added. "If I were the pilot, I'd just say to myself, 'there's nobody alive down on that beach,' and go back to my base."

"That's not the way it works. They keep looking for a long time—days and days."

9

For hours Todd listened for the sound of chopping blades to return. If he moved to the cave entrance to hold out the backpack, he would have to get down from the ledge into deeper water. Over by the cave mouth, if one of those big breakers crashed, the withdrawing suction of air and water might pull him out of the cave. Besides, how would he hang the backpack out the entrance so it could be seen by the pilot? If he heard the helicopter returning, would he be able to move fast enough?

Heidi tried to keep talking and smiling, and then she lapsed into silence again. It was afternoon now, and they were beginning to doubt that the helicopter would return.

Todd stood beside Heidi in the corner of the cave, forming a bulwark against which she could not fall down. His own knees were beginning to feel weak. He worried that Heidi might slump down, and he

137

would have to hold her forcibly above water level. He told her stories—the plots of movies he had seen and books he had read. He recounted the trouble he and his friends had been into at scout camp—how they had nailed kids' shoes to the floor and put hermit crabs in their beds. He kept giving her pep talks.

"The water level is really going down," he said with forced brightness. "The worst has got to be over. We just have to hang on a little longer, and the water will go back where it belongs." Beneath his optimism, his heart ached for getting Heidi into such a hopeless plight. He remembered how she had returned happily for the binoculars yesterday morning. And now she was trapped, bedraggled, and dispirited—and maybe doomed. Todd was bad luck for her, that was for sure. Every date he made with her either fizzled out or became a disaster.

The sea was not crashing as violently against the cliffs as it had done before, and Todd could actually see that the water level in the cave was lowering, for he watched the notches on his jacket zipper and could see that more of them were exposed. If he and Heidi could only hold out—keep their heads above water until the weather cleared. If only they didn't have to spend another night in the cave.

Then, over the sound of the sea, Todd heard again, in the distance, the faint chopping of helicopter blades.

"Heidi!" he yelled. He shook her to bring her wide awake. "You've got to stay on your feet. I think the chopper is coming back. I'm going to hang out the backpack."

"Okay," Heidi said with a faint smile. Todd was afraid to leave her. She didn't seem to have enough strength left to keep standing.

As Todd moved down the ledge, he could feel the

icy water moving on his chest. Stepping down from the ledge, it was up to his chin, and it was hard to walk, for the heavy salt water buoyed him up. He thought it must be like this to walk on the moon. The backpack was soaked with water. Todd wondered if it would stay up. It might get waterlogged and sink. He could hear the noisy motor of the helicopter approaching, and he braced himself against the wall of the cave mouth to keep from getting sucked out into the sea. Then he held the red backpack out as far as his arm could reach, trying to keep it on the water's surface. A wave washed it back into the cave. It wouldn't be seen. The helicopter was very close, and a swell of water passed through the cave mouth, covering Todd's head, and then the water receded with a strong tow that snatched the backpack from Todd's hand and carried it out into the sea.

Todd gulped and snorted out a noseful of water. It hurt. "Well, that didn't work." Todd dog-paddled back to Heidi. He was reluctant to leave her unguarded. "Your leaning post is back," he said, mustering up one of his biggest grins.

"Listen, Todd," Heidi said, her deep blue eyes coming wide open. "It's the helicopter."

"Yeah, it's passing by again."

"It's slowing, Todd. Listen."

"Hey, maybe—maybe that pilot did catch a glimpse of that backpack." They peered out the entrance.

"Todd, it's floating around out there. Can you see it? That red is so bright against the gray." Ducking his head down, Todd could see the surface of the water and the red canvas backpack being tossed around on the swirling surface of the ocean. They could hear a change in the pitch of the rotor blades.

Todd and Heidi looked at each other, and a burst

of hope exploded between them. Todd hugged Heidi close. A charge of energy suddenly animated them both.

"What do we do now?" Heidi asked.

"As soon as I'm sure the chopper is investigating this cave, I'm going out."

"Do you think we can make it?"

"For a few minutes, probably."

The noise of the helicopter increased.

"Come on, Heidi. I took livesaving last summer, only we never tried out our skills in a stormy sea."

"Me, too. At camp. I can swim pretty far—when I'm not so tired."

Todd and Heidi made it to the cave entrance, treading water for part of the way. Heidi was wearing her backpack.

"You should have left that behind," Todd scolded. "It might get heavy and drag you down.

"Let me go first," Todd added. "I'll yell if it looks like the helicopter is going to do anything."

Todd swam out of the safety of the cave into the rough sea, trying to make his way through the waves. He saw the helicopter hover and veer sideways. The pilot had spotted him and was lowering a sling. Todd turned back toward the cave. "Come on, Heidi, we're about to get rescued," he yelled. Todd tried to return to the cave mouth to help Heidi, but a wave parted them, and he could see Heidi's head emerge from the cave. She was fighting the rough seas with all the energy she had left, after being submerged for hours in the cold salt water.

The sling dangling from the helicopter flailed in the wind as the big craft hovered overhead. Todd tried to swim near it to hold it steady so that Heidi could pull herself up, but she wasn't making it. Her head disappeared below water, and Todd, his over-extended body fired with a desperate burst of energy, stroked toward her through the tempestuous water.

The helicopter moved sidewise like a giant insect above them, and from somewhere out of the layers of gray clouds another helicopter came into view. Todd saw the large letters on its side: "Channel 6 On-the-Spot News." The first helicopter lowered its altitude as Todd found Heidi, grasping her head under one arm. It had been a lot different doing lifesaving in the Blossom Valley High pool. The helicopter pilot skillfully maneuvered the sling toward the struggling pair. Heidi was not helping. She was just plain out of it, and Todd shoved her through the loop of the sling as he fought the waves. Seeing her motionless form being pulled up into the helicopter's side opening, he thought about his own precarious position. A big swell lifted him up then, and he couldn't swim against the force of the breaker that was rising behind it. He might as well give up. There was just so much a guy could take. The wave hurled him against the granite cliff.

When Todd came to, there was a confusion of noise from the rotor blades and someone's anxious face was above him. He wasn't in the water anymore. There was a dry blanket around him.

"This kid has come to," somebody said. Todd realized he was inside the helicopter. Somehow, they had gotten him in there.

"Where's Heidi?" he yelled wildly.

"She's over here. She's okay, but in shock."

Todd painfully turned his head and saw a blanket-wrapped figure over which somebody was working— a paramedic or something. He gave a deep sigh and relaxed. Everything about him hurt. Even that sigh had hurt. The helicopter chugged on through the dense gray sky, and then Todd heard the blades change pitch again. They were coming down. Todd felt a soft thud as the craft hit the landing pad.

"You seem to be all right," the paramedic told Todd. "You're one tough kid! And so's your girl-friend there. We're just going to take you over for a checkup. Your family has been notified."

The helicopter doors swung open, and Todd was whisked out of the chopper into a waiting ambulance. A man ran beside him, focusing a camera on him, and somebody yelled, "How do you feel?" Somebody else shrieked, "How deep was the water in the cave?"

"What was it like in the cave at night?"

"How did you happen to get into that cave?"

"When did you first learn you were trapped?"

"Lay off. The kid has been through quite an ordeal," the paramedic said to the swarm of report-ers. Todd had not been able to say anything, because the press people were all talking at once. He felt himself shoved into the ambulance, and the door closed with a slam. They were on their way again. Night was falling.

Todd looked over at the motionless blanket that held Heidi inside. "Is she okay?" he asked.

The paramedic nodded. "She's just suffering from exhaustion and exposure. She'll come out all right."

Todd felt terrible, thinking of what had happened to Heidi. He remembered her startling, luminous beauty when he had first seen her, and then the way she had ended up after a date with him. All salty and water-soaked, with her bubbly animation zapped out by the storm.

"Your family will probably be up to the hospital before long," the paramedic said after a while.

Todd thought about Sandy and Aunt Margaret. He would just as soon they wouldn't come. Aunt Margaret was fluttery and excitable, and Sandy was nobody to have around in an emergency. And he was in for it when his dad got back from Denver. Despite Todd's resolution to stay out of trouble this year, this was the worst he had ever been in. Bad enough to be on the TV news. Everybody and his dog would know it. It was really humiliating.

At the hospital Todd was prodded and probed, and more reporters appeared, pelting him with questions. Heidi had been taken to another room, and he didn't see her anymore. It felt good to be warm. Everything Todd had on now—one of those funny hospital outfits and plenty of blankets—was warm, and he was starting to feel like himself again. They brought him some broth, and the reporters even took pictures of him wolfing it down and asked him how long it had been since he had eaten and how it felt to be drinking broth.

"When will this be on TV?" Todd asked.

"Probably not until the eleven o'clock news, and maybe on the six o'clock news tomorrow," somebody said. Every insignificant move Todd made seemed to be of interest to these characters.

Then Todd was surprised and shaken to see his mom and dad appear. Both looked drawn and agitated. His dad was panting, as if he had run down the corridor. His mom gave him a hug and kissed him anxiously, and some cameramen were around taking pictures of it. The cameramen made Todd's dad uneasy.

"I brought you some dry clothes," his mother said. "They told us we could take you right home."

"I thought you guys were in Denver," Todd said.

"We were, but Aunt Margaret got the news to us, and we came at once."

"Gee, I'm sorry it wrecked your weekend."

"We had Friday and Saturday. Everyone was going to be leaving on Sunday, anyway, and the important thing is that you're all right."

"I feel fine. Maybe have a little sniffle. When I

first got here, my hands were all shriveled up from being in the water all night. Like prunes. But now they're okay." Todd held up his hands for their inspection. He was surprised that his folks were not raising Cain with him for getting into such a mess. But instead, they were being nice to him and were glad to see him.

"I left the car over by the beach," he said cautiously, getting into his dry clothes and shucking the hospital garb. Someone had collected the wet clothes he had been wearing when he was rescued and put them in a plastic bag.

"Uncle Ed and I will get the car after we get home," his dad said, as if it were of no consequence.

"Uncle Ed? Is he here?"

"Aunt Margaret called him and he came right out, after he heard the news."

"What about Heidi? Did someone come to get her? Is she all right?"

"When we came in, we asked at the desk about her and were told she couldn't be seen. But I would assume her parents got the same messages we did."

"I wish I could see her before we leave."

"I guess you can't. We'll have to get going. Uncle Ed and Sandy are waiting in the car."

"We thought you were dead," Sandy said as they got into Uncle Ed's car. "On the eleven o'clock news they said you might be. They had all these pictures of different disasters in the storm and one of them was you and your girlfriend. They said your abandoned car had been found on the cliff, and you and she were missing and feared drowned. The reporter even came out and got your yearbook picture to show on TV, and your girlfriend's was shown, too."

"Sandy, that's enough!" Todd's mother said sharply.

"Vicky was staying over last night, and we both cried. We never even went to sleep. Aunt Margaret didn't either. She called Uncle Ed and Mom and Dad, and she was waiting for them to get here. She was crying practically all the time until Uncle Ed came."

"Well, Todd doesn't have to hear all about that," Uncle Ed protested.

"This morning, everyone was calling up because it was in the paper. Right on the front page there were pictures of you and your girlfriend. Steve and Art even came over, and a whole lot of people called up. You know who even called up? The principal of the school. Everyone thought you were dead. There was a police car here, too, and the officers were asking us how tall you were and what you had on, but we didn't even know what you had on because you had left so early. Vicky was really freaked out. She was calling up all her friends to tell them about it, but Aunt Margaret made her get off the phone, so in case anybody found you they could call us."

"Sandy, will you shut up?" Mr. Roberts exclaimed irritably.

"Gosh, I didn't know there was such a flap at home," Todd mumbled.

"Steve and Art call all the time to ask if we have heard anything yet. They are pretty shocked."

"I'm sure Todd is anxious to get some sleep and doesn't want to hear any more about it," Mrs. Roberts said anxiously. Todd was leaning back against the corner of the backseat with his eyes closed.

"You know who else even called up? Andy Pearson," Sandy said in awe. "I answered the phone when he called. He's the champion debater. The pastor of the church came by this morning just before Mom and Dad came back and Uncle Ed and I were leaving to get them at the airport. We took Vicky home on the way, and she was so upset she left her overnight case and her stuffed unicorn at our house. They're still there. Vicky probably doesn't know you're alive yet. She said she was going to hit the sack the minute she got in."

"Well, you're going to hit the sack yourself, young lady," Mrs. Roberts admonished. "You are wound up like a watch spring.

"Todd is going to take a hot bath and get right into bed," Mrs. Roberts announced. "Todd, you haven't a bit of color in your face."

"And you smell like seaweed," Sandy grimaced. "Oh, I forgot to tell you. Right about six o'clock yesterday the guy at the pizzeria called to find out where you were. He was really mad."

"That's enough, Sandy," Mr. Roberts scowled.

When they drove up in front of the Roberts home, there was a van out in front and some cameramen waiting for them.

"This boy is worn out," Mr. Roberts told them. "He's barely able to talk."

"How does it feel to be home?" a reporter asked.

"What were your first thoughts when you saw your son alive?" another reporter was asking Mrs. Roberts.

"We have to get him to bed," Mrs. Roberts replied.

"I feel like my knees will cave in," Todd mumbled.

Sandy preened before the camera. "When I saw my brother, I decided I would never quarrel with him or invade his room again. While we thought he was dead, I wished that I hadn't bugged him so much."

Mrs. Roberts swept Todd into the house, leaving Sandy and Uncle Ed out in the yard with the reporters.

"You must be starved," Mrs. Roberts said. "I'll fix you something while you bathe."

"Not right now, Mom," Todd said. "They gave me

some kind of broth over at the hospital. I only want to sleep."

After a hot bath, in his pajamas and under some warm blankets, Todd heard Sandy calling her friend, Vicky. "Guess what, Vicky. I might be on the news tonight," she began, as Todd drifted off to sleep.

Todd didn't awaken until the middle of the afternoon of the next day. The rain and clouds had dissipated, and sunshine was streaming into his room. He felt ravenous, so he leaped out of bed and pulled on his robe. He ran downstairs.

"These youngsters sure do bounce back in a hurry," Aunt Margaret exclaimed, giving Todd a hug. "Well, Todd, you dropped off before I got a chance to see you yesterday. You sure gave us a fright!"

"There weren't any phones in that cave, or I would have let you know we were okay." Todd grinned.

"You look a hundred percent better today, Todd," his mother said.

"Yeah, I guess I'll live," he said. Miraculously, nobody seemed to be mad at him. He guessed it was because they had found out what it would be like if he wasn't there.

His mother and Aunt Margaret prepared a huge brunch for Todd. As he downed a plateful of scrambled eggs and sausage, Danish pastries, and fruit, he began to think of Heidi. She would be all rested, too, and he would call her. It seemed to Todd that the episode in the cave had happened weeks ago. Sitting in the sunny kitchen, with the light streaming through the dotted Swiss curtains, Todd felt that the nightmare in the cave and the struggle in the stormy sea were events he had only heard about— something that had happened to someone else, but not to him.

And yet part of it had been a good dream. The part where he had kissed Heidi, and they had sort of agreed to be in love. Hadn't they? He had kissed her a lot, as he remembered, until they were too wiped out to care about kissing.

Was she still going to care that much about him when they weren't isolated and trapped in that cave? Todd would soon find out, for he would call her and see if she could go out with him this weekend. Todd would book her up for all her free time—the Valentine dance, and everything. Thinking about Heidi being his Valentine date sent a surge of excitement through him. He bolted down the rest of his Danish pastry and ran upstairs to take a shower. Then he would call Heidi, and their romance would begin in earnest.

But as Todd emerged from the shower, he could hear a babble of voices downstairs. Some of his friends had come over after school, and he quickly pulled on some clothes. He would have to wait to call, because he didn't want to be rushed when he talked to her.

He could hear Steve's voice and Art's, Janine Anderson's and some others. As he hurried down, they were all waiting at the bottom of the stairs for him.

"Hey, it's the TV star!" Steve yelled, and everybody started cheering, and there was a hubbub of excited chatter.

"Yeah!" Art screamed. "Me and Steve and Connie were sitting around at Sarah's watching the eleven o'clock news night before last, and they were telling about this wild and fantastic storm that was hitting the coast and this damage and destruction, and they showed these pictures of you and this really cute girl, saying that your car was out on the road and that they suspected you had been lost in the storm."

"You could have heard a pin drop! We all just looked at each other. We were making some popcorn, and I couldn't even eat any," Sarah said.

"I was over at the arcade playing Pac Man," Ken Garcia said. "So I didn't even hear about it until I got home. My mom was pacing the floor and waiting up for me. 'Did you hear what happened to your friend, Todd?' she goes. I go, 'No, what?' And she goes, 'He's been drowned.'"

Steve had his arm around Todd, and they all went and sat down, and Mrs. Roberts brought them a liter bottle of Coke and some glasses and a bowl of pretzels.

"So what happened to you, anyway?" Sarah said.

"We went up into this cave to eat lunch . . ." Todd began.

"Wow, who was that beautiful girl you were with? I said to Steve, 'Did you ever see that girl?' and he didn't know her either." Art whistled.

"Wow," Steve echoed. "She was some dish. Where did you ever meet somebody like that?"

"Knock it off!" Todd said, a little scowl appearing on his face. The moments when he had held the exhausted Heidi up in the corner of the cave returned to him with all their pain and intensity, and he felt a big gap widening between him and his friends. He didn't really want to hear all their chatter, and he kind of tuned himself out.

"Who was she, anyway? She doesn't go to our school, does she?" Ken Garcia persisted.

"Her name is Heidi," Todd said, wishing they would all go away so he could call her. Janine Anderson shot him a sympathetic glance. She had not said anything at all.

"Where did you meet her?" somebody asked.

"I'll bet Todd doesn't even like to remember all this," Janine said, giving Todd a conspiratorial wink.

"My mom heard a newsbrief this morning saying

149

that you guys had been found, and she could hardly wait till school was out to call me. I was over at Steve's, and she called me there, and then Steve called Art, and we called all these other guys and decided we would come over and find out what happened," Ken Garcia said.

"I even called Craig over in Berkeley. He had been feeling bad about you all day. Was he ever relieved to find out you were still alive!" Janine added.

Todd's thoughts wandered to Heidi again. He wondered if her friends had all converged at her house, and if that guy Joe was over there. As soon as all these people had gone, he would call her and find out. Even if these were his best friends, he was kind of getting a headache listening to them and was looking forward to their leaving.

"It's starting to cloud up again outside," Connie said.

"Yeah, that sunshine was only temporary. There's supposed to be another storm hitting the coast tonight," Art announced. The wind began to wail outside.

Sandy and Vicky came in with a gust of rain. "It's starting again," Sandy said, making a face. "Is it time for the news? I might be on it. They took a picture of me and Uncle Ed out in the yard. It was Channel 6."

Sandy and Vicky settled themselves among Todd's friends and helped themselves to sodas. Todd felt a surge of unease. He felt that he wasn't really here, but was off looking at everybody through a telescope.

"Hey, right. Maybe they will have something on the news about you being rescued," Steve said.

"The news starts at five-thirty on Channel 6, and it's almost that," Sarah said.

Todd hoped they would not show him in the

hospital pajamas and drinking broth. In fact, he hoped that he would not be on the news at all. He didn't want to hear any more about it. A memory of the scent of brine and seaweed, and of being cold and wet all night, swept over him and made him feel slightly dizzy.

"They're starting," Sandy said, settling herself expectantly beside the TV.

There was a story about some trouble in Central America and then about disagreements in the Middle East. Then the announcer said that devastating storms were battering the Northern California coast.

"This is us," Sandy said with satisfaction.

The scene of a portion of Highway 1 that had been closed came on the screen, and then a picture of some rubble that had been a pair of beach houses.

"And in a dramatic rescue, two teenagers were plucked by the Coast Guard from a cave where they had been trapped all night."

"This is it!" Steve screamed.

The camera showed a picture of the Coast Guard helicopter and its sling, and you could see the two heads in the water and even the red backpack floating around.

"That backpack was how we let him know where we were," Todd said. "We tossed it out."

The camera showed Heidi missing the sling and Todd pulling her out of the waves and getting the sling around her.

"In a heroic gesture, Todd Roberts, seventeen, risked his own life to save that of Heidi Holmstrom, his sixteen-year-old companion. Knocked unconscious against the cliffs, Roberts was then brought in by Coastguardsman Bill Pendleton." They watched the Coastguardsman being lowered to grab Todd, who seemed to be foundering near the cliffs, and then they were both pulled up into the belly of the helicopter.

"Gosh, I didn't even know that happened," Todd said. "What a creepy feeling it gives you to see yourself on TV."

The news switched off to a fire in San Francisco.

"I didn't even get on it. They came clear out here to take pictures, and then didn't even show them," Sandy complained.

"They called you a hero!" Janine exclaimed. "You were, too. You could just as well have grabbed the sling yourself as to shove your friend into it."

No I couldn't, Todd thought, still feeling detached and looking at his friends as from a distance. They would never understand what it had been like down there, or how deep his feelings for Heidi had become during that time in the cave. It wasn't an experience most kids his age would understand.

"Todd, you should write that Coastguardsman a thank-you letter," said Mrs. Roberts, who had come in to watch the news. "What was his name?"

"Bill Pendleton," somebody remembered.

"I'll write it down. You drop him a note tomorrow."

"Heroic!" Steve breathed. "Wow!"

"Mom, do you think they'll show the rest of those pictures on the eleven o'clock news?" Sandy whined.

"I hope not," Mrs. Roberts scolded her. "I hope the whole incident's over and can be forgotten."

"I agree," Aunt Margaret said. "That was absolutely the most nerve-racking night of my life."

"But it only lasted a few seconds," Sandy complained. "You couldn't even tell who Todd was. They could have showed a lot more."

"I hope Craig was watching the news," Janine said. "He'll flip when he sees that rescue."

Todd wondered if Heidi had seen the news. Maybe she would know how much he cared for her if she could see what had happened.

"Todd, you look feverish," Mrs. Roberts said. "I think we better get you back to bed."

"Maybe we all should go," Janine suggested. "Todd is probably very tired."

"Yeah, we should let the hero get rested up," Art agreed.

"I already slept a long time," Todd said, "but I'm not quite back to normal." He was anxious for them to go so he could call Heidi and hear her voice and know that she was okay.

10

When his friends had disappeared down the street, Todd lunged for the phone. "I want to hold a *private* conversation," he said to Sandy. His adventure in the cave must have invested him with some authority in Sandy's eyes, for she went right upstairs.

Heidi's mother answered the phone, and Todd could hear Jamie and Jackie in the background.

"I'm afraid Heidi can't talk now, Todd. She's quite sick. It's pneumonia, in fact, and we have to keep her very quiet. You youngsters did give us quite a fright! And how are you recovering?"

"I'm not sick, just tired," Todd told her. "But I wondered if I could come over and see Heidi sometime."

"You better call me at the end of the week—Saturday or so—and we'll see how she's doing. We'll check with the doctor."

"Gee, I really feel bad that she's so sick. Be sure to tell her I called," Todd said, and he hung up morosely. Heidi's mother didn't seem to be mad at him about the whole episode, but he needed to talk to Heidi and see if she still felt the same way about him as she had in the cave. She dominated his thoughts. He didn't want to think of anything but Heidi. He cared more about her than he ever had about anything in his life. He wanted to see how it felt to have his arms around her when she was warm and dry and happy.

The next day, when Todd went back to school after a day's absence, he was mobbed by people who wanted to hear all about his adventure. Even people he didn't know well asked him about it: teachers, freshmen, the ladies who served in the cafeteria, the people who worked in the office. Everybody had to hear the details, and Todd had to repeat the story again and again.

"I think I'll make myself one of those sandwich boards that has the whole story on it, and I can wear it around and nobody will ask me any more questions," Todd said to Art as they went down the corridor.

"Yeah. It's getting repetitious," Art agreed. Somebody went by them and yelled at Todd, "That was some gorgeous chick you spent the night in the cave with." He raised his eyebrows and gave Todd a knowing grin.

Todd's mouth set in an angry line. "I'd like to pound that guy into the pavement," he said to Art.

"Well, they had these pictures of you and her on TV, and everybody was remarking on how you had this glamorous secret girlfriend that nobody knew, and everybody was wondering how you got together with her."

Todd had reached the door of the physiology room, and he had to go in to his class. He kind of liked his role as a mystery man, but he didn't care for people making remarks about Heidi. After school, he went to the stationery store and bought her a get-well card with a humorous message and some comical shorebirds cartooned on it. She would get a kick out of that. He drew a balloon over one of the birds' heads and wrote in it, "I love you."

It was an eventful week at school. Janine had to give her speech in the assembly on what it was like to live in Uruguay. When the principal opened the meeting, he mentioned Todd's adventure, saying that the school was glad to have its senior class president back after he had given them such a scare. Everyone whistled, cheered, and stamped on the floor. Todd felt embarrassed to be so conspicuous.

Then the principal introduced Janine. She began to talk about the street vendors who put out stalls on Sunday at what was called La Feria Dominical. At this Sunday fair, they sold oranges and grapefruit, chickens and ducks, books, flowers, cheese, pictures, and many other things. They even had a hot-dog stand there, she said. She told about the parks in Montevideo with lakes and swans, and about the old, baroque government buildings with fancy ceilings, pillars, frescoes, and statues. She told about the marvelous beaches at Punta del Este. There were two political parties in Uruguay, she said, the Blancas and the Colorados, but they didn't do much because a military junta ran the country. Meat, woolen and leather goods were the main products in Uruguay, she went on. Watching her, Todd thought how she had changed since they had gone to the Homecoming dance together last year. They had been a couple of gawky kids then, and now they were both practically adults. Janine had been halfway across the world, and he was not only president of the senior class, but had had this narrow escape and had been on TV. And both he and Janine were in love with really neat people. Last year, they wouldn't have dreamed that all these things would happen to them. It made them quite a lot more interesting than some of their classmates who led more humdrum lives. Todd was glad he and Janine were such good friends.

After Janine talked, the exchange student from Finland told about the impressions he had of life in California and told something about the different customs in his country.

Todd had to hold another meeting of the senior class. They would iron out the details of the Valentine dance, get reports from the graduation committee, and hear how the school volunteers were doing.

Before the meeting, Steve cautiously approached Todd. "Sarah wanted me to let you know that Jennifer had been sort of expecting you to ask her to the Valentine dance, since she has been doing all this work on it. She has spent practically all her time since the beginning of the year planning the decorations and getting the prizes. Before the dance, they're going to have to blow up hundreds of red-and-white balloons. It's probably going to be the greatest Valentine party the school has ever had. Jennifer has six people working on her committee, and every week they meet over at Jennifer's to make sure everything is getting done. That's a lot of work itself—just having those meetings, where she furnishes the refreshments out of her own money. And with you being president and Jennifer being in charge of the party, and since you were her date for her own New Year's party, Sarah said it seemed logical that you would pay Jennifer back for all the effort she's gone to by inviting her to the Valentine's dance, especially since Marty Redfield asked her to go, and she turned him down, assuming that she would be going with you."

"Well, gosh," Todd said. "I had already planned to take Heidi to that dance—you know, the girl from Orchard High I was trapped in the cave with. Ever since we decided to have that dance, I have planned on it. And so I don't know how Jennifer got the idea that I was going to ask her, when I've never really asked her for a date at all. It's not that there's anything wrong with Jennifer. She is a really okay person and good-looking besides. But she's not my type, and I've already got this commitment."

"Sarah will throttle me," Steve complained. "And Jennifer might be so insulted she'll quit her job and wreck the party."

"She wouldn't do that! Not after all that work."

"But how would you feel if you did all this work and didn't have a date with the guy of your choice for the dance you had worked so hard on?"

"She will have a date," Todd promised, "but it won't be me."

"She won't just go out with anyone," Steve scowled. "It better be somebody good, or my name is mud. I kind of promised Sarah that I would fix it up for Jennifer with you."

"Well, you've got to get Sarah to tell her that I am really hung up on Heidi, and there isn't any chance of my getting over it. And meanwhile, I'll fix her up with somebody she will like."

"You'd better."

Todd approached Ken Garcia after they had the meeting and all the progress reports were in. "Hey, Ken," he said. "Since you and I are the president and vice-president, I thought we ought to make sure that everybody who has worked on the Valentine dance has a date. And since I heard Jennifer Baines, the head of the dance committee, doesn't have a date yet, I thought that you and her . . ."

"Jennifer Baines! I would think that she would be the first one to have a date! Besides, I already asked somebody."

Todd began to worry. He didn't really have a date himself. Maybe Heidi wouldn't even want to go to a dance where she didn't know anyone but him. Yet it was inconceivable that Todd could enjoy a Valentine dance with anybody but Heidi. He ached to see her. On Friday, he called at the Holmstroms' again, but she was too sick to have company. The doctor thought she would be out of danger the next week. "Why don't you plan to come over on Saturday, Todd? I'm sure Heidi would love to see you then," Heidi's mother invited. On Saturday, then, Todd would ask Heidi to the Valentine dance. He wanted to do it in person, not on the phone, because, of course, a kiss was a natural accompaniment to such an invitation. The idea sent all kinds of wild impulses through him.

The burden of getting a suitable date for Jennifer Baines hung over Todd constantly. After all, people who went into politics had to keep everyone happy or, at least, thinking they were happy.

Todd spied Quentin Pierce, the singer, going out to the parking lot that afternoon. Quentin had been the leading tenor in the school musicals for the past couple of years, was a terrifically handsome guy, and was kind of an idol of the girls. He was noted for playing the field—hardly ever dating anyone more than twice. He had agreed to sing a couple of romantic songs at the Valentine dance, so he could be considered a member of the organizing committee.

"Hey Pierce, are you all ready for the Valentine bash?" Todd yelled.

"As ready as I'll ever be," he answered. "I'm planning to sing some oldies: 'My Funny Valentine' and 'Love Is the Greatest Thing.' Then if anybody wants to make any requests, I'll sing whatever they ask."

"That sounds great. Have you got a date yet?"

"Have I got a date? Good question. Let's see. Did I ask anybody?" Quentin got out a little appointment book. "Oh, I guess somebody asked *me*. In fact, somebody invited me over for dinner before the dance, and somebody else invited me for after-the-dance refreshments at her house. How will I juggle that one? I better get that straightened out. Thanks for calling it to my attention."

"Maybe you should turn them both down and say you have to hang out with the dance committee that night. That would solve your problem."

Quentin considered the solution and then looked back at his appointment book. "Well, on the other hand, I've never been out with Marybelle Williams before. I think I'll accept her invitation for dinner."

It was when Andy Pearson came over to show Todd some correspondence he was carrying on with a cap-and-gown rental company that Todd got the idea of pairing up Andy and Jennifer. It was an interesting combination—Andy being this very serious and intense student and Jennifer a frivolous social butterfly.

"You got a date for the dance yet?" Todd asked.

"The dance? You mean the graduation party?"

"No, of course not. That's months off. The *Valentine* dance."

"Oh, the Valentine dance! I hadn't thought much about it. I've been so busy, not only with the graduation arrangements, but also boning up for the debates. All these preliminaries to the championships. That's one reason I've been trying to get all the commencement details worked out. I may get terribly busy later on and won't have time to handle anything. I might even be doing some out-of-town travel."

"Gee, you're really organized, Andy. You're always thinking ahead."

"A guy has to, if he's to accomplish his maximum potential."

"But gosh, give yourself a break, man. Have a

little fun. You don't mean to tell me you aren't even *going* to the Valentine dance?"

Andy grimaced. "It really wasn't on my list of priorities."

"But we were hoping all the officers and committee heads of the senior class would be there. We have certain gifts for them and wanted to introduce everybody."

"Oh, in that case, I'll make it a point to be there. If it's an official duty, I wouldn't want to be conspicuous by my absence, though I've never been a devotee of dances."

"You owe yourself some recreation. All work and no play, you know. I thought maybe we would have some kind of arrangement where the officers and committee heads would sort of pair up as dates and we could all sit together. I wondered if maybe you could be partners with, say, Jennifer Baines."

"Jennifer Baines! Isn't she in charge of the whole party?"

"Yeah, she'll be pretty busy, but therefore she needs to have a date with somebody who's really organized."

"You think it would be okay with her?"

Todd surveyed Andy Pearson. Andy was a very nice-looking guy, basically. He was just too serious and intense. A workaholic type. He needed a bit of loosening up, and Jennifer was the sort who might accomplish that. Todd made up a white lie; sometimes it was necessary. "I heard she was kind of a secret admirer of yours. Only I'm afraid she thinks you're too intellectual to be interested in her."

"Jennifer Baines, eh?" Andy looked rather bemused. "There's an old maxim that opposites attract, and perhaps this is the proof of it." Right before Todd's eyes, Andy's scholarly manner gave way to a more relaxed and speculative expression. His eyes acquired an adventurous glint.

"You better ask her right away before somebody else does," Todd urged. "She would be really disappointed if she accepted another date and then you asked her."

"Oh, then you aren't making the arrangements?"

"I could, only I think Jennifer would appreciate a direct invitation from you more."

"Jennifer Baines!" Andy said again in wonder. "Of course. I'll take care of it right away."

Todd felt a little like Cupid as he saw Andy striding purposefully down the corridor in search of Jennifer. He crossed his fingers and hoped it would work out. But since he had gotten Andy interested in Jennifer, he ought to try to get a date for Betty Babcock. That wouldn't be so easy.

But when he sounded Betty out, he found there was no problem.

"Miss Pratt, the librarian, and Mr. Hansen, the playground supervisor, have bought tickets to the dance for all the volunteers, and we're all going to meet there and make it a kind of group date. Did you know that Pratt and Hansen are going to the dance themselves? There's a rumor they might announce their engagement there."

"No kidding!" Todd exclaimed. Suddenly he thought of Heidi. Would they, too, be engaged in the distant future? But that was crazy. He didn't even have a date with her yet! He could hardly wait for Saturday to get that settled. Just the thought of seeing her made his senses tingle.

On Saturday, Todd dressed with care to go to the Holmstroms'. He put on a new sport shirt that he had been saving for special occasions and shaved more closely than usual so that he wouldn't scratch Heidi when he kissed her. He splashed on some musky after-shave before grabbing his jacket and going to get the car keys from his dad.

"None of these two-day excursions," his dad cautioned.

"Yeah, I've learned my lesson," Todd told him. "I'm just going over to see how Heidi is. After all, I haven't seen her since the storm."

"You take it easy with that girl, Todd," his father advised. "She seems to get you into some difficult situations. I should think you could get interested in one of the girls around here instead of chasing all the way out to Berryville."

"Aw, Dad, none of it was her fault. Besides, there aren't any girls around here like Heidi. You don't know how smart Heidi is. Nobody over at Blossom Valley is as good-looking as she is, either, or so much fun. And she has this really fabulous family."

"Well, Todd, I'm afraid you might be idealizing this girl because she lives so far away and you don't see her every day."

"I've seen her plenty. That's the way she really is."

"I'm afraid you'll lose your sense of perspective. It's all right for you to be friends with this girl, but I hope you won't get too intense, and it looks as though you're headed in that direction. At your age, that can lead to trouble. I might say it already has."

"That was just a freak accident, Dad. Gosh, you would never find anybody with more common sense than Heidi. You ought to be glad I picked somebody like her."

"You are too young to 'pick' anybody, Todd. You ought to be going around with a lot of different girls."

"I'm only going out there to invite her to the Valentine dance, not to propose to her."

"Well, see that that's all you do. There's just no point in getting too involved right now."

"Gosh, Dad, quit making such a big deal of it. I'm only going over there to see if she's okay."

"Don't stay over there long enough to worry us."

Todd turned the ignition switch so hurriedly that he flooded the engine and had a hard time starting the car. His dad glowered at him. "It beats me how you passed driver training," he said.

Todd finally got the car going, and it was a relief to be pointed in the direction of Berryville. There was no sign of a storm today. After all the rain, the fields were turning green, and there was a sprinkling of mustard flowers under the trees in the orchards that lined the route to Heidi's house. Here and there an almond tree bloomed. It was so great to be headed toward a meeting with Heidi on such a sparkly day that Todd began to sing in the car. He was a pretty croaky singer, though, so he quit and turned on the radio instead. He got excited thinking about taking Heidi to the dance. Everybody had been remarking on how cute her picture was on TV. Wait till they see her in person, he thought, with her shiny, spectacular hair, and those dimples in action! They would be bowled over! He could hardly wait to stroll in the door with her. He would have his arm around her waist. He was going to use some of his pizzeria money to rent a tuxedo. Not everybody would be wearing a tux, but Todd had never worn one, and since he was president, he had a right—or maybe even an obligation—to do so. Heidi didn't even know he was president. That would be a welcome surprise to her. She was going to find out that, in addition to all the things she had already admitted she liked about him, he was a real mover and a shaker out on the dance floor. The Valentine dance was going to be the *coup de grace*. Heidi would be his forever—to kiss and hug whenever he felt like it, which would be all the time. . . .

At long last he reached the Holmstroms' long drive. It was getting to be familiar. He drove along beside the weathered rail fence that stretched down to the house, and he smelled the fresh scent of acacia and almond blossoms. Four big white ducks crossed the road, gabbling among themselves. He loved Heidi's place. It was very rural looking. The Holmstroms were pretty different from the people in his neighborhood—more natural and easygoing. Jupiter was perched on the rail fence, and at Todd's approach he sailed off majestically into a field of mustard flowers, his lovely blue-green train dazzling against the yellow. Todd caught his breath. There was a magic surrounding Heidi, and he was enchanted by it.

Out in front of Heidi's house there was a car parked, a blue station wagon. As Todd maneuvered himself into a parking place, the Holmstroms' front door opened; someone came out and crossed the front porch. It was Joe, Heidi's perennial boyfriend. He looked big and hulking and a little ill-tempered. He had on a green-and-white snowflake-pattern ski sweater. He stopped at the top of the porch steps when he noticed Todd parking his car and viewed him through narrowed eyes.

Todd felt uncomfortable, like an intruder under Joe's scrutiny. Then he remembered his words with Heidi in the cave:

"You like me better than him, then."

"Can't you tell by now?"

And then he and Heidi had kissed each other. He wished Joe were not looking so belligerent and that he had something to carry, like some flowers for Heidi, so he could just stroll past Joe as somebody going to call on a sick friend. But Joe was definitely glowering. As Todd closed the car door and approached the steps, Joe stood solidly on the porch, his chin thrust out inimically. You would have thought he was the Holmstroms' watchdog.

"You're the guy that got Heidi trapped in that cave," Joe accused as Todd's foot reached the first step of the porch. His voice was menacing.

Todd did not like the way Joe had phrased his accusation.

"I was in there with her, yeah," he corrected.

"She could have died because of you. I wouldn't think you'd have the nerve to come over here," Joe growled.

"Mrs. Holmstrom invited me," Todd countered. He had reached the porch now, and Joe confronted him. Todd was taller than Joe, but Joe was heftier.

"Heidi and I go steady," Joe growled. "We'd appreciate it if you would butt out and quit bothering her."

"Speak for yourself," Todd said coolly. "That's not the way I heard it from Heidi."

"So you weaseled your way into her dad's field trip and then got her to go out with you once. But now that she sees how you bungle things up, she wouldn't do it again. So why don't you just split and go back under the rock you crawled out from. You're not wanted around here."

"I didn't come over here to talk to you." Todd was unnerved by Joe's manner. Joe had moved back so that he was standing against the Holmstroms' front door to bar Todd's entry. Every nerve in Todd's body was strung like a bowstring ready to unleash an arrow. Behind the door that Joe barricaded was the luminous Heidi. All Todd's love was brimming up inside, ready to be poured out for her. And now this jerk was in his way. Todd had an overpowering impulse to sock his fist right into this guy's face, but he wasn't going to be as crude as Joe.

"Okay, I dare you to open that door and let Heidi decide which one of us she wants to see," Todd challenged, implying more confidence than he really felt.

Joe made the first move. He lunged for Todd, twisting his shoulders around until he had pinned him against the wall of the house and then landing a fist in Todd's stomach. Todd reacted quickly to the shock and pain. He took a deep breath, and a big surge of energy and anger propelled him as he leaped at his attacker, throwing Joe off balance and knocking him to the floor. He landed on Joe, pummeling him until Joe's powerful body twisted itself to roll Todd over and retaliate. They made an awful racket on the board planks of the porch, and once, as Todd rolled over to give Joe a punishing punch, he could see the Holmstroms' alarmed faces at the windows. The struggling adversaries rolled over the porch and crashed down the front steps into the dust of the yard. The four peacocks squawked and skittered away, and then Jupiter approached the pummeling pair with his tail fanned out threateningly.

The front door opened and Heidi appeared. "Stop!" she cried. "I want you both to stop that fighting right now."

"Heidi, you stay out of this. Go back in the house. I'll settle this fracas!" It was her father's voice—not his usual, congenial, lecture-style voice, but an outraged roar, to which Heidi responded instantly. Todd heard the door close as he rolled over in the dust, landing a frenzied fist into Joe's face as they continued to tumble and pound. Todd could not get a good perspective on what was happening. All he could do was try to keep on top and to land more punishment on Joe than Joe could on him. Todd jackknifed his knee up and gouged it into some part of Joe.

Then both the pugilists gasped and came to their senses. They were being doused with a strong spray of water. Todd separated himself from Joe and got to his knees. Joe pushed a clump of wet hair away from his eyes and looked in surprise to see Dr. Holmstrom aiming the garden hose at them.

"This is what we used to do when I was a kid to break up a dog fight," Dr. Holmstrom said with distaste. "And since you boys haven't got enough judgment than to act like animals, it'll do for you, as well. Now I want you both off the premises, and I don't want to see you around here anymore. You don't need to phone. Heidi will not be accepting any phone calls from such thugs, and neither of you will be welcome here in the future."

"But I haven't even gotten to see Heidi," Todd protested. "I've been waiting for two whole weeks."

"Well, you'll wait a lot longer, for in the future we're restricting her company to civilized human beings," Dr. Holmstrom said. "Joe, I've warned you before, and my patience has run out. I want to see your rear license plate disappearing down that road as soon as possible, and for good."

Dr. Holmstrom's usually amiable mouth was set in a grim, relentless line. He meant business. Joe had turned and was ambling sulkily toward his car. He got in, but didn't leave. He kept looking back to make sure Todd wasn't going to remain and wheedle his way in to see Heidi. As soon as he saw Todd in his car, Joe slowly pulled away. Todd went even slower. He didn't want to be too close behind Joe.

11

Todd drove home in confusion, his thoughts flying like leaves in a dust devil. He had actually caught a glimpse of Heidi, and then she had been snatched from him, without his being able to say a word to her. He had heard her voice, alarmed and disapproving. And now Todd was in bad with Dr. Holmstrom. What was the use of going to State now, if the professor already had an unfortunate impression of him? Everything was ruined—including his clothes. He was covered with mud, from rolling in the dust and then being hosed. He felt degraded. It had been unfair. If only he had started out for Heidi's ten minutes later, he might have been with her now. He would have missed Joe. None of this would have happened. Todd felt bruised, mistreated, and outraged. His arm hurt, and there was a sharp stinging in his right cheek. He felt it with his hand. His skin had been scraped on the rough boards of the porch.

Todd parked the car in back of the house when he

got home. He was a mess and hoped to sneak up to his room and change before anyone saw him. But it was impossible.

"Whatever happened to you?" his mother asked, clearly astonished.

Todd mumbled that he had slipped into a puddle, which was partly true. He didn't want to admit he had been in a fight or to talk about it. "I better go up and change," he said.

As he shucked his muddy clothes and cleaned himself up, Todd became angry at Dr. Holmstrom. After Todd had driven all the way to Berryville, he had not been allowed to see Heidi. He imagined the scene ending as it should have. Mr. Holmstrom should have come out and said; "Get off the premises, Joe. You have been hanging around Heidi too long, and you're annoying her guest." Then he would have ushered Todd in to see Heidi. And Heidi would have been grateful to Todd for rescuing her from the obnoxious Joe.

Todd was not going to give up. He thought over his strategy. Maybe he should wait until Dr. Holmstrom had cooled down and then phone.

"Well, you didn't stay over there very long, I see," his dad commented when he came downstairs. "Good. You can get caught up on the yard work you didn't get around to doing last week. You mowed the lawn, but you didn't trim around the edges. And I thought I told you to cut back those shrubs out by the garage."

The world was a pretty unfair place. Everyone seemed to be on Todd's back today. He took out the clippers, did the detested chore on the lawn, and then trimmed the shrubbery by the garage so it didn't obstruct the walk. As he carried the clippings to the trash can, he thought of how soon the Holmstroms had forgotten that he had sort of rescued Heidi. Even Heidi seemed to have turned on him. She certainly hadn't run out and protested her dad's treatment of him. She could have plunged through the door and thrown herself between him and Joe. "Get lost, Joe, it's Todd I love," she would have said.

After all, his dad should have appreciated the fact that Todd worked at the pizza parlor and earned his own spending money, so he shouldn't have to do this yard work.

To make the day even more unbearable, Todd could see Vicky and Sandy coming down the street. Now he was going to be plagued with that insipid Vicky's incessant flirting. But instead, Vicky and Sandy confronted him with superior, smug glances.

"We won't be bugging you tonight!" Sandy crowed. "We both have dates."

Vicky simpered. "Mine is with this really cute guy, Bobby McCord." She looked at Todd triumphantly.

"His sister was Homecoming Queen last year," Sandy added. "And I have a date with his friend Chuck Ellis. Chuck is on the junior varsity swimming team."

"Oh? Are Mom and Dad aware of this?" Todd knew that Sandy had not been allowed to date yet.

"We're just about to tell them. But I know it will be okay, because it's Cindy Rasmussen's birthday party we're going to. We are all going to Hamburger Heaven and then to the movies."

"Did you ask those guys, or did they ask you?" Todd asked.

"Kind of both," Vicky giggled, as they ran into the house, and Todd felt a strange emptiness. As much as he had loathed Vicky's coquettish attitude toward him, it hurt his ego to have the admiration of his kid sister's friend jerked away, especially today. Everybody had a date but him. Everyone was paired off, but he had no one. He had found the girl of his dreams, but she was inaccessible to him.

"What's that scrape on your cheek?" his mother asked when he went in to get ready for his job at the pizzeria.

"I told you. I slipped in this puddle, and that's where I hit."

"You better put some antiseptic on it before you go. By the way, how is Heidi doing?"

"She's okay," Todd answered in an uncommunicative mumble, and he was off to the pizzeria.

Todd prepared his dough and got ready to put on his performance out in the display window. His big grin came out crooked tonight. He wasn't in the mood. Sometimes he turned away from the specta- tors. The pizza crusts were not whirling as high as usual. One of them landed on the floor, and the owner came over with a scowl.

"What's the trouble?" he asked.

"I guess I don't feel so hot. I'm not really into it tonight," Todd said.

"You never have been the same since that storm," the owner commented. "Maybe I *will* switch you over to the ovens. One of the other guys has been wanting to try out the crust routine."

So Todd moved over to the ovens, where he could slather the crusts with sauce and pile them with cheese and onions, anchovies and mushrooms. Over there, he didn't have to play to the crowd; as he prepared the pizzas he could be as glum as he wanted, and he could think of Heidi. He wondered what she had done after her dad had sent her friends away. He could tell she was well again. He had just caught a glimpse of her, but in that brief moment, her radiance had come across to him. He felt drawn to her as if he were a planet orbiting the sun. He would never be free from aching to see her. What was she doing tonight? In spite of her dad, there was no law against calling her, so as soon as there was a lull in the orders, Todd went to the pay phone and dialed her number, which he now knew by heart. But nobody answered.

Had she gone out with her family to dinner, as they had done before? It was pretty clear that she was not out with Joe—but if Joe was out of the picture, would all those other Orchard High guys move in? There would probably be such a rush on her that Todd would get muscled out. He was already exiled from her house. Anger rose in him. He was not going to stay exiled. He would go out there and fight for Heidi again. In general, though, he had a record of being unlucky in love. Last year, he had lost Janine Anderson to Craig Matthews. Only what he had felt for Janine wasn't even a smidgen of the love he felt for Heidi. Heidi was the great love of his life. He never stopped thinking of her: stroking a peacock, running down the beach, climbing a cliff, explaining about the length of bird beaks, making friends with an otter, being a part of a meadow full of flowers, laughing, kissing. She was unforgettable. The longing to be with her was like a fever. When he went to sleep at night, he was thinking of her, schemes tumbling about in his head about how to get together with her. When he woke in the morning, the memory of her was the first image in his consciousness.

At school the next week, for practically the first time in his life, Todd felt lonely. Every time he tried to get together with his friends Steve and Art, they were always on their way to meet their girlfriends and didn't have time for him. Between his physiology and English classes, he ran into Jennifer Baines. Time was running short. It was almost Valentine's Day. Jennifer brought him up to date on the latest developments and arrangements.

"You're doing a fabulous job," Todd complimented. "I'll bet there has never been a Valentine party like this one."

"You'll never know we're in a gymnasium," Jennifer said confidently. "And there's not going to be a dull moment. The music will be great, and there will be all kinds of things going on to keep people on their toes and mixing around. We will count on you to be master of ceremonies when the door prizes are given out. I should tell you, though, in case you had any ideas, that you don't need to count on me to be your partner at the dance. It just so happens that I have a date with Andy Pearson!" Jennifer shot Todd a look of victory and revenge.

"Andy Pearson!" Todd said in mock surprise. "I didn't know you and he were that friendly."

"Surprising things happen around Valentine's Day!" Jennifer looked very happy and proud to have a date with Andy. Andy must do the job of asking a girl to a dance with the same thoroughness and finesse with which he did everything else.

"Yeah." Todd smiled a kind of dispirited smile at Jennifer.

"I suppose you'll be bringing your girlfriend from the storm over to the dance," Jennifer said casually, as if she didn't care too much.

"I don't know," Todd evaded. "She doesn't really know anybody but me over here at Blossom Valley. She might not care to come, so I might go stag."

Jennifer raised her eyebrows. "It would be pretty strange for the president of the class to come stag, but I already promised Andy."

"Sure. I understand," Todd said. The Valentine dance got to be a chief topic of conversation at school. Since Jennifer had done such a great job on the arrangements, practically everybody in the class was coming, even kids who weren't usually worked up over dances. As Todd walked home one afternoon, he wished he could get more into the spirit of such a great dance. Before he had met Heidi, he would have been the most hyper person in the class over the party, because dancing was something he got a real blast out of. But this time, without Heidi, he couldn't get interested.

Todd saw Janine Anderson walking ahead of him toward home. She, too, was all alone.

"Janine!" he called. "Wait up!"

She turned and smiled at Todd and stood while he caught up with her.

"How's it going?" he asked.

"Okay, I guess."

"You guess? That means it's slightly doubtful."

"It's the midwinter doldrums, I guess." Janine smiled faintly. "Plus an anticlimax. Nothing seems very exciting this year. I guess last year was too much—the trip to South America and all."

"And a certain guy isn't over here at school anymore," Todd reminded her with a sly grin.

"Yeah. I miss him a whole lot. It's terrible."

"He'll be back for the Valentine dance, I hope."

Janine made a face. "Afraid not. That darn basketball schedule. They have a game that night, so I guess I'll be at home with a good book."

"It's the pits to be hung up on somebody who's off at another school, isn't it?" Todd commiserated.

"Yeah. Especially when he has to play basketball every weekend. Anyway, I hope you'll all have a good time at the Valentine dance. Are you taking your girlfriend from Orchard High?"

"Well, actually, there have been some complications," Todd told her. Somehow, Janine was a person Todd felt like confiding in, and he poured out the whole story of the fracas with Joe on Heidi's porch and the subsequent banishment of them both.

"So as it stands now, I'm whatchacallit—*persona non grata*—over at the Holmstroms'." Todd smiled a sad little crooked smile at Janine.

"Why, I never heard of such a thing!" Janine exclaimed. "After you rescued her! And obviously, it was all the other guy's fault!"

"I guess her dad also feels I got her into that mess, so that cancels out the rescue. Gosh, Janine, I've got to think of a way to see her. It's the first time in my life I've really been miserable."

"You've always been the cheerful one," Janine reminisced. "Remember last year, you were the one who kept everybody in stitches? Remember, when you did your presidential campaign on your skateboard and cracked the whole school up? Our Spanish class was everybody's favorite because of all your jokes and tricks on Mr. Rodriguez."

"Sure. Only now things are more serious since I met Heidi and have lost her. Nothing is as funny anymore."

"Come on, Todd, don't be so gloomy. Why don't we go over to the Creamery and get an ice cream cone?"

"Right on! That's an inspiration!"

On the way to the Creamery, Janine and Todd recalled how Todd had gotten Janine a job at the Creamery last year, and how busy they had been filling cones on Homecoming Day.

"It was unbelievable how you used to do that trick of flinging the ice cream down the counter into a cone," Janine laughed.

"Yeah, it was fun." Todd and Janine ordered their cones—a chocolate almond swirl and a pineapple orange sherbert, and they strolled toward home licking them.

"Janine!" Todd exclaimed. "I just had one of those great ideas I'm famous for."

Janine laughed, and her eyes sparkled with interest. "What are you cooking up now, Todd?"

"How about you and me being a twosome for the Valentine dance? Why should we both be lonesome and miserable? Look. Craig trusts you with me, or he would have never asked me to bring you over to Berkeley. And we are dynamite on the dance floor together. Remember? And the president of the senior class really shouldn't go alone to the Valentine dance, should he? So even if we're both in love with other people, why shouldn't we have a good time?"

"Why not, indeed?" Janine's smile lit up her whole face and even seemed to bring a glow to her reddish-gold hair. "Let's do it, Todd! I'm just itching for some fun!"

"We'll wear a deep groove in that gymnasium floor," Todd predicted.

"Craig calls me almost every night," Janine said. "I'll tell him we're going to the Valentine dance together, and he'll be glad. He feels very guilty that he can't come over more often and that I'm not having much fun this year."

"Fun is going to be the name of the game on Valentine's Day!" Todd exclaimed. But he couldn't help thinking of Heidi and wishing that his original plan to take her to the dance had worked out. Anyway, nobody—not even Heidi's father—could keep him from sending her a valentine. He went to the stationery store and looked over all the valentines. He finally settled on an old-fashioned one with one of those lace doilies that sprang up when you took it out of the envelope. It just had a heart and a cupid on it, and it said simply, "Be My Valentine." Before he put it in the mailbox, Todd wrote on it, "I'll love you forever."

12

When people asked Todd whom he was bringing to the dance, he always told them he had a mystery date, and Janine was going along with the spoof, telling everyone she was staying home that night because Craig couldn't come.

"Craig seemed to think it was okay for us to go together, but he sounded a little unhappy that he wasn't going to be there," Janine told Todd on the day before the dance. "He really wanted to come."

"You're lucky that you heard from him," Todd said. "I sent Heidi this huge valentine, but I haven't heard one line from her. I guess she got just as turned off as her father by that fighting."

"We're going to have a good time anyway," Janine smiled.

The morning of Valentine's Day, Todd opened his bedroom curtains to see what kind of weather it was going to be. Even though Heidi wasn't going with him, he was still obligated to wear the tux he had reserved at the rental store, and he was hoping he wouldn't get rained on when he wore formal attire for the first time.

Todd peered out into cloudless skies. It was a good omen. Then, lowering his gaze, he saw something electrifying. It was one of those double-take things—what did they call it? *Déjà vu:* something he had seen before, repeating itself. It was undoubtedly Jupiter Holmstrom! His train trailed long and luxurious behind him on the lawn as he picked out invisible bugs and morsels from the grass.

Todd erupted from his door into the hall. "It's that peacock!" he yelled. "It's back!" Sandy appeared at the bottom of the stairway as he bolted down.

"I'd change out of my pajamas if I were you," she said with a sly, knowing air. "Jupiter may not be alone."

"The hens are here, too?"

"Let's just say Jupiter may be with a chick. Anyway, don't go out in your pajamas."

Todd hurriedly ran back to put on his jeans and T-shirt, picked up a handful of puffed rice, and went out to view Jupiter.

"What—" Todd saw that an envelope was tied around Jupiter's neck. He approached cautiously. Jupiter flew up onto a low branch of an almond tree. He was breathtaking among the blossoms with his iridescent blue-green tail hanging elegantly from the bough. Todd crept up on him slowly and silently. He could see Sandy watching from the kitchen window.

Todd grabbed the envelope, as Jupiter squawked and sailed from the bough, then ripped the side off the envelope. Todd pulled out the contents with trembling excitement. It was a valentine! The picture showed a peacock with heart-shaped eyes on its tail. It simply said, "Be My Valentine, Love, Heidi." Todd let out an ecstatic whoop, which sent the alarmed Jupiter skittering up to the roof.

"How did she find such a valentine? And how did she get Jupiter to bring it over here?" Todd said to Sandy, who had appeared in the yard.

"It was a put-up job, I think. I thought I saw a suspicious-looking station wagon pull up in front of our house, and this peacock got out. I don't think it was driving, though. There's something funny going on here."

Todd looked frantically around, and from down the block, he watched the Holmstroms' station wagon slowly approach and park in front of the house. The door opened, and Heidi jumped out and ran into Todd's arms. She turned up her radiant, laughing face to receive Todd's eager kiss as Sandy watched delightedly.

"Oh, Heidi," Todd said. "I thought I was never going to see you again."

"Oh, come on, Todd!" Heidi was still laughing at her trick. "How could that happen to us?"

Todd held her close. He was never going to let her get away again. "Those weeks I didn't see you were torture," he said.

"For me, too. Right away, I convinced Dad that the fight wasn't your fault. He knew it all along, of course, because he knows Joe so well. And we were both glad that the occasion allowed us to get rid of Joe once and for all. Only Dad wanted to teach me a lesson—not to be so careless. So he wouldn't let me see you till today. He couldn't resist Valentine's Day."

"You sure have a romantic way of delivering your message."

"Are you going to be my valentine?"

"Sure. As long as it's mutual." They kissed, and couldn't seem to stop.

Then they heard the sound of Todd's mother clearing her throat in the doorway.

"Todd, you haven't had your breakfast yet.

Wouldn't you like to bring your friend in for some pancakes?"

"I could eat a hundred of them!" Todd yelled, propelling Heidi into the house with his arm still tightly around her and her gaze fixed happily on him.

Todd's mother got acquainted with Heidi, and then Sandy sidled in, contemplating Heidi's clear beauty with awe. Todd felt very proud to have Heidi meeting all his family, and he could see that they were as entranced with her as he was.

"I know it's short notice, Heidi," Todd said anxiously. "but we're having this Valentine dance at school tonight, and I've been hoping you would go with me, only your dad said he didn't want me calling, so I kind of gave up."

"One of my ulterior motives in sending my messenger Jupiter out today was so that maybe I could wangle a Valentine date," Heidi admitted, the deep blue pools of her eyes holding his. "I'd love to go to your Valentine dance."

Todd's widest grin appeared, and Heidi's dimples played tantalizingly about her mouth. Todd and Heidi just gazed at each other, and Mrs. Holmstrom and Sandy thought of some errands they had to do upstairs. When they were gone, Todd and Heidi melted together again.

In the midst of all this incredible happiness, Todd suddenly remembered his arrangement to take Janine to the dance.

"What's the matter?" Heidi asked in alarm as she saw Todd's ecstatic mood change to a stricken expression.

"Gosh, I just remembered. I promised to take this other girl to the dance."

"Another girl!" Heidi looked puzzled and hurt.

Todd put his arm around the back of her chair reassuringly. "It's not like it sounds. It's just Janine. She goes steady with this college guy who has to play basketball, so he can't come. And since I thought I couldn't go with you, and Janine and I were both feeling lonesome, we just decided to go together instead of staying home. She knows how I feel about you."

"Oh, well, then," Heidi's face resumed its happy radiance. "Why can't we make it a threesome?"

"I guess we could," Todd said reluctantly. It would be awkward to escort two girls, especially when one of them was Heidi, to whom he wanted to give his undivided attention.

"Let's do it," Heidi said. "I wouldn't want you to disappoint her."

"It will probably work out." Todd sounded doubtful.

"I have to get home," Heidi said. "I promised Dad I wouldn't stay long, and suddenly I'm going to a Valentine dance. I'll have to find something to wear."

"You could wear your oldest jeans and you'd still be the most beautiful girl there."

"Come on, flatterer. Help me get Jupiter in the car. We'll see who can catch him first."

Jupiter was up on the roof, looking for insects in the rain gutters. Todd got out the ladder and brought him down to Heidi. He stuck his head in the car as she began to drive off and said, "I don't know how I can wait—how long is it? Eight whole hours till I pick you up tonight!"

Todd planned that he would first pick up Heidi, and then they would drive by Janine's. He wondered if he should warn Janine of how his plans had changed. If he did, he was afraid she would back out, and he would feel bad about her sitting home alone on Valentine's Day, after they had talked so much about the fun they were going to have.

Yet, he didn't want to shock her by coming by with another girl. So he would just amble by her house and tell her in a really low-key way just what had happened, and how Heidi wanted to meet her, so they would all go together.

Todd set out down the street toward Janine's, and coincidentally he saw Janine approaching up the street.

"I was just coming down to see you," he said when they met.

"Small world. I was just coming over to see you." Janine's eyes were animated, and she was in a carefree, happy mood. The sun was shining in her red-gold hair, and she was wearing her biggest smile.

"Something wonderful has happened," she said. "Craig has sprained his elbow."

Todd looked bewildered. "Wonderful?" he asked.

"Yes! It really doesn't hurt much, he said. But it has put him out of the basketball game, and he's coming down for the Valentine dance. It isn't going to make any difference, Todd. Craig wants the three of us to go together. You know how he is about rock music. He only likes slow dancing, and you're so good at the fast ones that we decided I can take turns. I knew it would be okay with you."

"It's more than okay, because I have news for you!" Todd exulted. He kind of felt the presence of that little fat archer, Cupid, because everything was working out like a charm. Todd told her about Heidi and Jupiter and the valentine.

"Unbelievable!" Janine laughed. "Simply incredible! I can't wait to meet Heidi."

"She said the same thing Craig did when I told her about our arrangement—that we should make it a threesome."

"I haven't seen him for three whole weeks," Janine said. "How can I endure until tonight?"

"Let's all meet over by the north door to the gym," Todd said. "That's where the valentine box with all the gifts and prizes will be."

"By the valentine box at a quarter of nine," Janine agreed, and they both turned and walked toward their respective houses.

"That's a lovely girl, Todd," his mother smiled. "I'm so glad you found such a nice girlfriend."

"It looks as if she's the one who found Todd," Sandy teased. "I saw it all. First, she let that peacock out, with the valentine around its neck. Then she backed down the street to a place where you couldn't see her car. Pretty obvious, if you ask me."

"She can be as obvious as she wants." Todd was all smiles, his head in the clouds. The feeling lasted all day and intensified when he was dressed in his tux and left to get Heidi. It was the evening he had been waiting for all his life.

Arriving at Heidi's house, Todd was welcomed by Dr. Holmstrom, who talked to him until Heidi was ready. He seemed surprised to see Todd looking so grown up and so elegant. Todd was even a shade taller than Heidi's father.

"Sorry about the little incident with Joe," Dr. Holmstrom said heartily. "We had all had just a little too much disturbance that week, and I'm afraid my nerves were showing."

"It's okay," Todd grinned. "I was pretty nervous myself."

"Tell me about this party you're going to," Heidi's dad said. "Heidi seems quite excited about it."

"She won't be disappointed," Todd said, telling her father about the decorations and the favors and the band, and how they were going to meet this star basketball player from U.C. Berkeley and his girlfriend. Then Heidi appeared.

"You kids have a good time," Dr. Holmstrom said, "and don't keep her out as long as you did on your last date!"

"I'll take better care of her this time," Todd

promised. Out in the car, he surrounded her with a close embrace and covered her face with kisses.

On the way, Heidi chattered about all that had happened to her since their adventure in the cave. He took her hand as they arrived at the Blossom Valley High gym, and they entered an enchanted world. The entire ceiling was covered with red-and-white balloons, and more balloons shaped like hearts and flowers stood like surreal plants, weighted down among the tables around the sides of the gym. The tables were covered with white crepe paper with bowls of red-and-white camellias in their centers.

Todd looked around for the valentine box. It was awesome. A giant-sized extravaganza covered with hearts, arrows, lace, and cupids. He saw Janine and Craig, holding hands and deep in conversation, at one side of it.

"Come on, Heidi, we're going to meet these friends I told you about." Todd propelled her over to the valentine box, and both Craig and Janine greeted Heidi with delighted grins.

"So this is the glamour girl Todd has been hiding away!" Craig exclaimed with exaggerated fervor.

"I've been hearing about nothing but Heidi, and at last we meet," Janine added. "And I can see how you lured Todd away from the Blossom High girls."

"Knock it off," Todd said good-naturedly.

Jennifer drifted by with Andy Pearson.

"I can't believe it, Jen," Todd complimented. "I didn't think such a transformation was possible." He introduced Heidi to Jennifer and Andy.

"It's not, unless it's Jennifer who's doing it," Andy said, his eyes glued on Jennifer. Todd reflected that he was a pretty good matchmaker.

"Listen, everybody, I have some news," Janine

185

announced. She looked lovingly at Craig. "I haven't even told Craig yet. I was keeping it a secret until tonight."

"Don't keep us in suspense," Craig begged.

"Okay. I just got my acceptance in the mail today from Berkeley."

Craig let out a yell and grabbed Janine in a joyous embrace.

"Wow! Just what we hoped for. We'll be together again! No more lonesome weekends," Craig exclaimed.

Todd put his arm around Heidi. The band was tuning up, and soon the action would start. Todd's feet began shuffling restlessly, and as the band went into its first number, his shoulders, elbows, and knees went right into it with them. He grabbed Heidi, and they were the first ones on the floor. A big yell and some catcalls went up from the rest of the party-goers, who formed a circle around Todd and Heidi as they danced.

"Todd!" Heidi complained. "I didn't know we were going to be on display." Heidi was light and lithe and graceful. She and Todd looked as if they had been dancing together all their lives.

"Why not?" Todd laughed. "You're like some kind of a pro."

"I love dancing with you, Todd. You're terrific."

There was a great surge of happiness in Todd's heart. It was an okay world.

Later, Todd kept Heidi with him when he introduced the class officers and announced the door prizes.

"Todd!" she scolded after he had finished, "you didn't tell me anything about yourself. Are you really the president?"

"Sure. But it isn't a big deal. Hardly anybody else wanted the job, and now that I have it I'm not sure I do."

"It seems pretty important to me. And you have all these terrific friends. I wouldn't think you would have bothered with me when you know all these neat people. Besides, I knew you were a good-looking guy when I first met you, but if I had imagined how handsome you would look tonight, I might not have dared to ask you to be my valentine."

Quentin Pierce had started singing "Love Is the Greatest Thing," and somebody was dimming the lights.

"I asked you first," Todd reminded her, drawing her close into the circle of his arms.

Three exciting First Love from Silhouette romances yours for 15 days—<u>free</u>!

If you enjoyed this First Love from Silhouette® you'll want to read more! These are true-to-life romances about the things that matter most to you now—your friendships, dating, getting along in school, and learning about yourself. The stories could really happen, and the characters are so real they'll seem like friends.

Now you can get 3 First Love from Silhouette romances to look over for 15 days—absolutely free! If you decide not to keep them, simply return them and pay nothing. But if you enjoy them as much as we believe you will, keep them and pay the invoice enclosed with your trial shipment. You'll then become a member of the First Love from Silhouette℠ Book Club and will receive 3 more new First Love from Silhouette romances every month. You'll always be among the first to get them, and you'll never miss a new title. There is no minimum number of books to buy and you can cancel at any time. To receive your 3 books, mail the coupon below today.

First Love from Silhouette® is a service mark and a registered trademark of Simon & Schuster.

First Love from Silhouette

THERE'S NOTHING QUITE AS SPECIAL AS A FIRST LOVE.

$1.75 each

1 ☐ NEW BOY IN TOWN
Francis

2 ☐ GIRL IN THE ROUGH
Wunsch

3 ☐ PLEASE LET ME IN
Beckman

4 ☐ SERENADE
Marceau

5 ☐ FLOWERS FOR LISA
Ladd

6 ☐ KATE HERSELF
Erskine

7 ☐ SONGBIRD
Enfield

10 ☐ PLEASE LOVE ME . . .
SOMEBODY Johnson

11 ☐ IT'S MY TURN
Carr

12 ☐ IN MY SISTER'S SHADOW
Dellin

13 ☐ SOMETIME MY LOVE
Ryan

14 ☐ PROMISED KISS
Ladd

15 ☐ SUMMER ROMANCE
Diamond

16 ☐ SOMEONE TO LOVE
Bryan

17 ☐ GOLDEN GIRL
Erskine

18 ☐ WE BELONG TOGETHER
Harper

19 ☐ TOMORROW'S WISH
Ryan

20 ☐ SAY PLEASE!
Francis

21 ☐ TEACH ME TO LOVE
Davis

22 ☐ THAT SPECIAL SUMMER
Kent

$1.95 each

23 ☐ WHEN SEPTEMBER
RETURNS Jones

24 ☐ DREAM LOVER
Treadwell

25 ☐ THE PERSONAL TOUCH
Cooney

26 ☐ A TIME FOR US
Ryan

27 ☐ A SECRET PLACE
Francis

28 ☐ LESSON IN LOVE
West

29 ☐ FOR THE LOVE OF LORI
Ladd

30 ☐ A BOY TO DREAM ABOUT
Quinn

31 ☐ THE FIRST ACT
London

32 ☐ DARE TO LOVE
Bush

33 ☐ YOU AND ME
Johnson

34 ☐ THE PERFECT FIGURE
March

6 brand new Silhouette Romance novels yours for 15 days—Free!

If you enjoyed this Silhouette First Love, and would like to move on to even more thrilling, satisfying stories then Silhouette Romances are for you. Enjoy the challenges, conflicts, and joys of love. Sensitive heroines will enchant you—powerful heroes will delight you as they sweep you off to adventures around the world.

6 Silhouette Romances, free for 15 days!

We'll send you 6 new Silhouette Romances to keep for 15 days, absolutely free! If you decide not to keep them, send them back to us. You pay nothing.

FREE HOME DELIVERY. But if you enjoy them as much as we think you will, keep them by paying the invoice enclosed with your free trial shipment. You'll then automatically become a member of the Silhouette Book Club and receive 6 more new Silhouette romances every month.

There is no minimum number of books to buy and you can cancel at any time.